THE

TRAILWALKER

ELLIE JORDAN, GHOST TRAPPER, BOOK THIRTEEN

by

J. L. Bryan

Published October 2020

JLBryanbooks.com

Acknowledgments

Thanks to my wife Christina and my father-in-law John, without whom I would be a full-time parent struggling to write at odd hours.

I appreciate everyone who helped with this book, including beta readers Robert Duperre and Apryl Baker (both talented authors themselves). Thanks also to copy editor Jason Sizemore of Apex Book Company and proofreaders Thelia Kelly, Andrea van der Westhuizen, and Barb Ferrante. Thanks to my cover artist Claudia from PhatPuppy Art, and her daughter Catie, who does the lettering on the covers. The cover model for this is Joslyn; her DeviantArt page is https://www.deviantart.com/twilitesmuse.

Thanks also to the book bloggers who have supported the series, including Heather from Bewitched Bookworms; Mandy from I Read Indie; Michelle from Much Loved Books; Shirley from Creative Deeds; Lori from Contagious Reads; Kelly from Reading the Paranormal; Lili from Lili Lost in a Book; Heidi from Rainy Day Ramblings; Kelsey from Kelsey's Cluttered Bookshelf; and Ali from My Guilty Obsession.

Most of all, thanks to the readers who have supported this series! There are more paranormal mysteries to come.

Also by J. L. Bryan:

The Ellie Jordan, Ghost Trapper series
Ellie Jordan, Ghost Trapper
Cold Shadows
The Crawling Darkness
Terminal
House of Whispers
Maze of Souls
Lullaby
The Keeper
The Tower
The Monster Museum
Fire Devil
The Necromancer's Library
The Trailwalker
Midnight Movie

Urban Fantasy/Horror
The Unseen
Inferno Park

Time Travel/Dystopian
Nomad

The Jenny Pox series (supernatural/horror)
Jenny Pox
Tommy Nightmare
Alexander Death
Jenny Plague-Bringer

Chapter One

"Guard rails should not be optional this high up," I said, palms sweaty as I white-knuckled the clunky, reluctant old van up the steep mountain road.

To our right, a high wall of overhanging boulders and massive, steeply leaning old trees threatened to kill us all, as the WATCH FOR FALLING ROCKS signs helpfully reminded us.

To our left, just beyond the occasional oncoming car, lay a steep drop, hundreds of feet down to the forest below.

Did I mention the rain? Because it was definitely raining, making the road slippery and blurring my view of the many forms of death lurking all around. Not even bothering to lurk, really, just standing out in plain view on both sides, waiting for me to make a wrong move.

I'm not a big fan of heights. It's not my greatest fear—
I mean, fire still exists—but it makes the VIP list, especially
since that one poltergeist nearly threw me off that balcony.

"You want me to drive?" Stacey asked.

"I'm fine," I lied, steering around another tight, blind
curve, doing my best not to scrape the van against a
protruding boulder.

"This is why I was saying my car might have been—"

"Yes," I said. Stacey had indeed offered to drive her
Ford Escape, a hybrid SUV actually designed for rugged
mountain driving, but I had turned her down. Back home,
it hadn't seemed worth the trouble of transferring all our
standard gear from the van to a vehicle that wasn't designed
for securely transporting a lot of sensitive cameras and
such.

I was starting to regret that decision.

We were hours from home, high in the Appalachian
Mountains. Vistas of early spring green surrounded us,
views that took my breath away, partly owing to my mild
panic attacks at the sight of enormous drops over the edge
of the slippery blacktop.

"Have you ever been up here before?" I asked Stacey,
mostly by way of distracting myself from my anxiety
regarding the steep and slippery road.

"Kinda. I've kayaked the Toccoa, which is a few miles
thataway." She pointed vaguely. "But that's about it. This
area looks like it might have neat hiking, though. If the case
doesn't pan out, we could still enjoy a couple days of
camping."

"Yeah, I suppose," I said, with no real intention of
doing that. Stacey had packed the van with an abnormal
amount of camping supplies because of where we were

going, but this didn't mean I would agree to engage in recreational use of it. Though sleeping in a tent can be preferable to sleeping in a house where an entity is feeding on the energy of the living, as evil entities tend to do.

People pretty much only call us about the evil ones.

"Here's the turn-off," Stacey said, and I slowed.

The crumbling wooden sign was barely legible, its support posts lost in overgrown brambles. Years of weather had nearly erased the words carved into the sign: CAMP STONY OWL. The arrow pointing up the dirt road was equally worn and hard to see.

More legible was the plastic NO TRESPASSING sign, red letters on black, stapled above the words and the arrow.

"Looks welcoming," I commented. It didn't, really, but I was relieved to turn away from the long drop on the other side of the road.

I turned, and the trouble started. The van had a difficult time slogging its way up the muddy dirt road, steeper than the paved one we'd just left.

"Did you ever go to camp as a kid?" Stacey asked me.

"I went to softball camp for a week one summer."

"But I mean *real* camp," Stacey said. "With canoes and archery and campfire singalongs—"

"Since my first response was 'softball camp' you can probably guess that I never went to that kind of—"

"I did! Camp Mizpah. They had everything. Hiking, arts and crafts, wildlife studies, photography. I was even in the chorus."

"Sounds like a busy summer," I mumbled, mostly concentrating on the muddy canal of a road. It finally evened out a bit, and the van made some progress through the woods.

"'Oh, Camp Mizpah, my friends so dear to me,'" Stacey began.

"Are you really singing—"

"'Oh, Camp Mizpah, faithful land and trees—'"

"How can land be—"

"'—good manners and loyaltyyyy—'"

I ignored her as best I could. The muddy road turned sharply, and I slowed. The road was barely wide enough for the van. If anybody approached from the opposite direction, we'd risk a head-on collision.

Another wooden, hand-carved sign stood past the bend in the road. It depicted a simple cartoonish boy and girl, their hands raised in a wave, the boy slinging a fishing pole over his shoulder like Opie in an *Andy Griffith* rerun. The characters were crudely etched, and might have been borderline cute in their day, but erosion had rotted off most of the boy's face and filled the smiling girl's eyes with moss. WELCOME CAMPERS! read the words above the creepy child figures.

"Seriously?" Stacey said. "So creepy."

"What, that doesn't give you happy childhood flashbacks?" I asked. "You didn't have moss-covered zombie kids at Camp Mizpah?"

"The closest thing was construction-paper monster masks. During craft time, obviously."

The mud track snaked through deeper, thicker woods with older trees.

We reached a tall, wooden stockade fence made of rough logs, like a fort from the 1700s, blocking any view of what lay within. A stockade gate blocked the road, with faded NO TRESPASSING signs stapled to it.

A six-foot wooden owl loomed beside the road, carved

in the same rough fashion as the other signs we'd seen. Badly deteriorated, perhaps gnawed by wild animals, its face and wings half rotted away, the giant horned owl looked like it had recently crawled out of its own grave. Faded letters were etched into its stomach: CAMP STONY OWL.

"He doesn't look stony to me," Stacey said. "More woody. And corpsey."

I honked, as the client had instructed.

We sat quietly for a while, soaking up the silence. I cracked my window to listen for any response. The air smelled like wet earth after the recent rain. Water droplets from soaked tree limbs overhead tapped the roof of the van like fingertips.

Water also dripped from the big dead owl, who regarded us with hollow, termite-eaten eyes.

The rain tapered off and finally stopped as we waited.

I honked again.

"Maybe they're gone," Stacey said after a minute. "Maybe they decided, hey, you know, this place is just too creepy-crawly even if you get rid of the ghosts, and we really shouldn't be having kids out here at all anyway, let's just shut it down."

"I doubt it," I said, honking a third time after another decent interval.

I was about ready to make my intervals a little shorter and less decent when the big wooden gate began to move, creaking and groaning as it swung inward.

More muddy road lay inside, leading through a foggy, gloomy forest tunnel of overarching limbs.

"Who opened the gate?" Stacey whispered.

I pulled ahead, my high beams doing little to dispel the shadows in the woods.

.

Chapter Two

Inside the gate, I stopped the van and looked back.

A woman closed the palisade-style gate behind us, latching it with a wooden board. Our prospective new client was tall, maybe in her mid-to-late thirties, her platinum hair tied in a ponytail under her cap. Her jeans and boots looked fairly new. Her baseball cap featured the blue Viking logo of Berry College. She waved as she walked over to us.

I lowered my window. "Hi there, I'm Ellie Jordan. Are you Allison?"

"Yep, I'm the one you talked to on the phone." She gestured down the road. "Just pull on ahead, park at the main lodge."

"Thank you."

The lady touched the brim of her ballcap and walked to her black Lexus SUV, a machine that likely handled the mountain roads better than our van.

I pulled ahead through the dark tunnel of trees, which widened into a gravel parking area at what I assumed to be the main lodge. We parked and got out, Stacey and I taking a minute to stretch and walk around after the five-hour drive.

Allison parked nearby and joined us. "Thanks for coming out. I know we're way off the beaten path. And the paved road."

"We're happy to come," I replied.

"It's a great place you've got here!" Stacey blurted out, looking around.

"Really?" Allison looked puzzled. "It's kind of a hideous wreck."

"Oh," Stacey replied, thrown off.

From what I saw, I had to agree with Allison's assessment. The main lodge was a wide two-story building, made of wood so heavy and dark it seemed to absorb the light around it. A sagging wraparound porch encircled the first floor.

"This campground has been closed for years," Allison said. "It wasn't my favorite of the sites we considered buying—not at all—but I guess it could be worse. My husband was set on it."

"Your husband Josh, right?" I pulled out my pocket notebook.

"Right. He's taken the kids to town for a shopping day. It's a long drive. That should give you some time to look around."

"Sounds good. So when did the trouble start? What was your first experience?"

"I never felt good about the place." She led us toward

the dark lodge, moving more slowly and reluctantly the closer she got.

As if changing her mind at the last second, she didn't lead us inside the lodge, but instead around to the back, following a gravel trail.

Behind the lodge was a sunken, sandy area with a fire pit large enough to barbecue a mammoth, ringed by tree-trunk benches and boulders for seating.

"Ooh, nice," Stacey said, nodding in approval. "You can fit a lot of happy campers around that. It reminds me of when we used to gather and sing our song at my own summer camp." She looked ready to break into song again, but I shot her a warning look.

"That's the idea," Allison said, sounding doubtful as she frowned at the fire pit. "The renovations aren't going as quickly as we'd hoped. New problems always come up. It's like building on quicksand."

"How long have you been working on restoring the camp?" I asked.

Allison trudged toward the back doors of the lodge like she was still reluctant to go inside. She stopped and looked off down one of the trails leading away from the fire pit and into the woods; maybe she'd heard something, maybe she was just thinking. "We closed on it about six months ago, after a year of shopping possible sites. I don't know why we bothered looking so long. Josh had his heart set on this one from the beginning. Personally, I was envisioning something a little more... not this."

"What were you hoping for?" I asked, since she'd fallen silent, still gazing down the trail, perhaps thinking about how life was an unpredictable twisting, turning path through a forest of uncertainty, perhaps not.

"I really connected with another place," she finally answered. "A farm with an amazing large brick house and some other nice buildings we could have expanded. I was imagining a performing arts center. Yoga. Maybe a science lab. Computer coding. Plus traditional activities, of course. There were apple groves, some gardens. The lake was nicer. The whole place was sunny and open. Not like..." She glanced down the trail again, a shadowy path under a dense, low cover of dripping tree limbs.

"Not so rustic?" I asked.

Allison gave a resigned laugh. "But Josh specifically wanted something rustic. And he's right about the old owl being a draw for the site. It gives us a real history and connection to the land, as long as we do our part to care for it."

"The old owl?" I asked.

"Nobody knows who made it. It's a neglected cultural treasure, thousands of years old."

Stacey and I shared a look. The big wooden owl out front, rotten as it was, couldn't have been thousands of years old. She must have meant something else.

"The old owl does give the camp a greater sense of mission, Josh is right about that. And this is all about the mission," she said.

"What mission?" I asked.

"To mold character. To give kids a place like earlier generations had. Get them away from their screen time and out into the wild, learning traditional skills. Playing with each other instead of video game characters. Building things with their hands. Making them into more confident and capable people."

"Wow," Stacey said.

"That's quite a mission," I agreed.

"My plan was to build a nice place where we could charge a lot, but offer scholarships," Allison said. "Let the high-income families subsidize some low-income ones. But Josh thought a more rustic environment was better for the mission. And he wanted to apply that hands-on character-building philosophy to our family, too. So we're all out here, Josh and me and the kids, doing hard labor to get this place open by June. I don't see it happening."

"It does seem like a big job," I said.

Allison stepped up onto the old porch of the lodge. "I suppose we should go inside," she said, as if she'd been sentenced to it as a punishment.

We followed her across the creaky boards of the porch, through a screen door, and into the darkness.

Chapter Three

"They call this Great Owl Lodge," Allison said. The walls had been freshly painted a rustic brown color that matched their original wooden hue; the tang of paint still hung in the air. The warped old hardwood floors had been recently scrubbed and polished.

A stone fireplace dominated one side of the room, with a life-sized owl carved into one end of the fireplace's tree-trunk mantle as if perching there. A semicircle of completely mismatched old sofas and armchairs faced the currently empty, cold fireplace.

"We brought in the furniture ourselves. This place was a wreck. I know it still looks like a wreck, but it's actually a big improvement."

"I like it!" Stacey said, glancing up at the heavy beams bolstering the ceiling. "It's got... character."

"Just about everything on the first floor had been

broken or chewed to shreds when we bought it," Allison said. "Some windows were wide open, and all kinds of animals had been through here. Maybe bears, by the size of the claw marks. The furniture, the walls, everything was torn up."

"You've done a great job." I stepped close to a wall filled with faded photographs, most of them black and white. The oldest showed boys and girls in military-style uniforms, canoeing, shooting arrows, marching in formation down a trail. The uniforms looked too hot for summer wear, with trousers for the boys, ankle-length skirts for the girls.

Near the baseboard were Polaroids; here, the thick uniforms and stiff, broad-brimmed campaign hats of early years had given way to 1970s-style short shorts and helmet hair. "It looks like this place has been here a long time."

"It first opened around a hundred years ago. My husband could tell you exactly, but it's old. He felt like it would give us a tradition to tap into." She shrugged.

"What was here?" I pointed to a noticeably empty square on the floor, less faded than the area around it, as though something had been there for many years.

"A horned owl," she said. "Preserved through taxidermy, but it still looked rough. And weird. I mean, it's literally a dead animal, and it was just sitting out here like a decoration. I moved it to the museum area."

She led us into a small back-corner office with two facing desks. One desk was chaotic, littered with notes and sketches scribbled on random pieces of paper. More random jots and scribbles, some on restaurant napkins, were pinned to a nearby bulletin board. The other desk was neatly organized, everything sorted into labeled trays, nothing out of place. A stack of crisp, white stationery with a horned-owl logo occupied one corner.

Allison walked toward the neat and organized desk, where a framed photograph offered my first glimpse at the rest of her family. Her husband Josh was smiling, strikingly good looking and wearing a nice suit, a big grin like a politician or a guy who's about to tell a joke you've heard a thousand times before, just before trying to sell you insurance or a used car.

They had three kids, two boys of middle or high school age and a girl who looked like she wasn't far out of kindergarten. The girl had dark eyes and seemed to glare at the camera while her brothers forced smiles.

"This is my desk," she said. "You'll, uh, have to excuse Josh's. He claims to have a special pattern of organizing his things, but we both know he actually just doesn't organize them. Anyway, I used to keep the windows open while I worked, if the weather was nice." She nodded toward two areas cloaked in floor-to-ceiling canvas curtains. "Now I keep them closed tight. I've seen something out there. And heard things."

"What kinds of things?" I opened the curtains, revealing two windows large enough for someone to step right through. Both were closed and latched.

"When I'm here working alone—I have to keep all the details squared away, you know, insurance and taxes and our costs. There are so many costs. So much depletion of our... our budget." She looked pained for a moment, but swallowed it back.

"Anyway," she continued, "the first time it happened, it was night and I was in here alone. I heard footsteps on the back porch. They came closer and closer to the side window there. They didn't even scare me at first, because I assumed it was Josh coming up from the cabin he'd been renovating.

"I even started talking to him, catching him up on what I'd been doing, but he didn't reply. The footsteps kept thumping closer and closer until they were right outside my window. We hadn't put in the screens yet, and the windows were wide open. A cold breeze rustled the curtains. A stray cold breeze by itself isn't anything unusual up here in the mountains, but something about it made me uneasy.

"I looked up, wondering why Josh hadn't answered me. I said his name and watched the window, but it was too dark outside to see anything. There was just solid black nothingness out there, but it made me think of that old saying about the darkness looking back at you. You know that one?"

"I do."

"When Josh didn't answer me, I started imagining some kind of, I don't know, wild man of the woods stalking around the place. Maybe the lodge previously had a squatter, or more than one, that the bank didn't know anything about. Maybe there was somebody else out here with us, somebody dangerous. Maybe this wild and crazy person had caused all the damage... and maybe he was still out here, watching us from the woods, resenting us for taking his home. That was what I imagined.

"So I got up, thinking I would close the windows, but I was too scared to actually walk over there. Without the screens, they may as well have been a pair of wide-open doors.

"I grabbed my letter opener." She took a long, thin blade from her desk and pointed it at the window. "My hands were shaking so hard I could barely hold it. I couldn't help feeling like someone was watching me from out there in the dark, someone I couldn't see. I kept thinking about how isolated we are, and how I'd always had a little bit of a bad feeling about this place..." She swallowed.

"What did you do next?" I asked, as gently as I could.

"I walked out." She turned and left the room. Stacey and I followed her back into the wood-paneled hallway, following the geography of her story. "I eased out of there one step at a time, and I didn't take my eyes off that window until I reached the hall, and then I ran."

She led us back to the big fireplace room and pointed at the panel of light switches by the back door. "That door was open a few inches. I had to force myself to walk over there. I turned on every last outdoor light, and I turned off the ones inside for good measure. Then I went to the fireplace to grab the poker, since I needed a better weapon than this." She wiggled the letter opener.

"Good thinking, Allison!" Stacey gave her a thumbs up, but this did not appear to cheer up Allison at all.

"Before I got there, I heard the front doors creak open." She turned and pointed the letter opener at the double front doors, visible down a short, wide front hall. "I jumped when I saw him. But this time it really was Josh, thank goodness. I tried to tell him what was going on, but I was so panicked it came out like gibberish."

"What was his reaction?"

"He was worried. We looked around, but found no sign of an intruder. He drove me to the caretaker cottage to stay with the kids, then came back by himself. I didn't want him to, but he said he had to lock up and make sure nobody was inside.

"I did my best to act normal in front of the kids, and anyway I was already starting to question myself. I could have heard any kind of noise out there and thought it was footsteps. It wasn't like I'd even been paying much attention. It could have been anything from a raccoon to a black bear on the porch. I wouldn't know the difference. I grew up in north Atlanta, in suburbs where you didn't see wildlife much bigger than a squirrel. All this roughing it out here is still new to me." Her face told me she wasn't necessarily enjoying it, either.

"Yeah, I'm definitely more of a city girl myself," I said. "Did your husband find anything when he searched the lodge?"

"Nothing. There was nobody here, at least not anymore. He left it locked up with all the lights on. He said that should help keep animals away. I knew he also meant people, like maybe trespassers, but he didn't say it out loud. We locked up our house tight that night, and every night since. We hadn't always bothered before that."

"Did you ever hear the footsteps again?"

"Oh, yes. Not just at night, either, although it's so dark around here under all these old trees, it always feels later than it is. Now I always work with the porch lights on and the windows latched."

"How many times have you heard them?"

"I don't know exactly. Three or four times out on the porch. Other times, I've heard them upstairs like somebody was clomping around the attic. I panicked then, too. At some point Josh stopped taking me as seriously. He told me it was probably the old building settling and creaking. Which I didn't believe. He started treating me like the wife who cried wolf. And I was questioning myself, too. I kept having to push it all down to act positive for the kids, because two out of three are already not happy to be here."

"Have they reported anything unusual?" I asked.

"Well, Shy immediately said she was seeing things, right after we moved in, but she's always let her imagination run away with her. She's always daydreaming and drawing wild things."

"That's your daughter?" I asked, thinking of the frowning girl with the big, dark eyes.

"Shiloh, yes. She's seven. Quiet as a mouse most of the time. But she has nightmares, and they got worse after we moved here. She's had a hard time adjusting."

"What has she seen?"

"She claims to see invisible people running around the cabins and sometimes down by the lake. The old people, she calls them, or the campers. And she sees a giant who walks out of the woods at night. And a herd of unicorns on the ropes course. And a fairy flying on a broomstick."

"Ooh, a witch fairy," Stacey said. "Neat. Imagine the outfits. And the shoes."

"And those are just a few examples. Shy isn't an outgoing kid—she makes Ephraim, my moody older teen, look like a chatterbox—but when she talks, it's almost always something made up. It's hard to know when to believe her."

"Do you think she's making it up?" I asked.

"Maybe not all of it. Not anymore." Allison looked like she wanted to say something else but held it back. She'd crossed the main room to the back door, and now slid the screen door aside and stepped onto the back porch. "Let's get out of here."

"Sounds good," I said, letting her take the lead. She'd mentioned seeing things when we'd talked on the phone, but maybe she didn't feel comfortable talking about that yet.

I followed her out into the gloomy afternoon, notepad open, ready to see more of this allegedly haunted campground.

Chapter Four

The fire pit behind the lodge, with its rings of log seats, seemed to be the camp's hub. Paths led off in different directions through the woods, marked with wooden signs so weathered they were illegible.

We followed Allison down a path that had been recently cleared. Weeds had been whacked down all along it, and masses of dead, shriveled poison ivy indicated someone had been at work with a sprayer. Overhead limbs looked recently pruned back, too, raising the canopy over the trails but not fully alleviating the gloom.

We emerged into a clearing arranged around a smaller fire ring. A cluster of cabins stood nearby, freshly restored. Flowers bloomed in the window boxes. I peered through one window, trimmed on the inside with starchy lace curtains. The cabin's interior was dollhouse-like: cheerful yellow walls with red trim, a ceiling fan that looked like a sunflower, butterflies painted on the white bunk-bed ladders.

"These are the girls' cabins," Allison said. "It's taken some work, but they're mostly done. New wiring and plumbing. New everything. Josh says the boys' cabins should stay a little rougher, because they'll end up that way anyhow, so we started those later."

"Is this where your daughter says she saw people?"

"That was the boys' area, over through those woods." She pointed down another trail that curved out of sight, presumably toward the less-restored boys' area. "And down by the lake, which is just past that."

"Let's have a look," I said. Allison nodded and started down the trail.

Stacey followed behind us more slowly, taking snapshots of the cabins, the fire ring, the brick bathhouse surrounded by raised garden beds ready for planting. Each cabin was freshly painted with a different cutesy animal—a rabbit, a bluebird, a chipmunk.

"This place is so fun," Stacey said. "I like how each cabin gets a different animal."

"Those were already there," Allison told her. "We added fresh paint and made them look a little friendlier. A mascot helps each cabin become its own little community. I think it helps kids feel more at home and gives them a special sense of identity. Their own little tribes."

We started down another path through thick woods. The way forward looked gloomy, more like a tunnel; the place needed a major trimming back of its canopy. A little more sunlight would have gone a long way.

Allison told us in detail about all the hard restoration work around the campground as we walked the path.

"Unfortunately, opinions about the work vary among the kids," she said. "Nathan, our fourteen-year-old, really has a knack for it. I think he likes the noise, the banging and hammering and drilling. And he's proud of himself when he finishes a project. He's like his father. Ephraim—he's the sixteen-year-old—not so much. For weeks, it was like pulling teeth getting him to help at all. Now he's more resigned to it, but he just doesn't have Nathan's spirit."

"And what about your daughter?" I asked.

Allison frowned. "Shy is... a little different. She tries to help but wanders off into her own little world. She's not being rebellious. I don't always understand the world inside her mind, to be honest. Here's the boys' cabins. Like I said, we haven't made as much progress here."

"This is definitely more rustic." There were a dozen cabins on the boys' side, not all of them restored yet.

Some of the cabins near the back were little more than shabby ruins. Allison led us to one of these, painted with a faded, peeling bobcat with an aggressive snarl. Allison hadn't yet repainted it into something friendly.

"That mascot is not so cute," Stacey said.

"All the cabin mascots here on the boys' side looked like this when we got here," Allison said. "Not exactly kid-friendly. I have to cuten them up as I paint over them."

The cabin door creaked and swayed in the wind, knocking against the cabin's outside wall. Allison stepped up onto the cabin's stoop and closed the door firmly, with the frustrated sigh of someone doing the same thing for the thousandth time.

"Josh left his tools here in Bobcat Cabin once, overnight," she said. "So he didn't have to haul them back and forth. When we came back the next morning, the door was wide open and everything had been knocked over or thrown around. We thought we'd been robbed! But nothing was missing.

"Josh said it must have been animals, maybe a black bear. Or maybe the world's biggest bobcat. 'My fault, I must have left the door open,' he said. He started leaving his things in Fox Cabin after that."

"So does Josh have a background in construction?" I asked, trying to get a clearer picture of these prospective clients.

"That's what he did in Atlanta, planned out communities for a real estate development firm. He designed really expensive neighborhoods, and the high-end shopping centers to go with them. That's what he got tired of doing, though. Insulated nests for rich people, he called them, but I thought it gave him a chance to create really beautiful things.

"But he wanted to do this instead. Go out in the woods, create something meaningful. And I support him. His heart's in the right place. He feels a calling. Maybe he could have spent a few more years at that job, and we'd have been a little more safe and secure, but he was working seventy hours a week. He would have missed these last few years with his sons, and he'd already missed most of them. It was a hard choice." She looked quietly at the dilapidated cabin, as if still feeling those hard choices. "I hoped it would bring us all closer."

She went quiet, and I took in the place. Like the girls' area, there was a bathhouse and a fire ring marked with stones—not as large as the giant ceremonial-sized pit out behind the main lodge, but just the size where campers could sit together, toasting marshmallows and telling secrets and ghost stories.

The cabin area bordered the woods. A steep hillside with several spindly trees formed a natural barrier that might help keep wayward boys from wandering too far—or maybe challenge them into the adventure of a treacherous climb into the wild places above.

Chapter Five

Most of what I knew about going to camp came from the movies, a scattershot of lame kid comedies, crass teen farces, and cheesy horror flicks. So far, this place was pretty well fitting my accumulated movie-based impression of summer camps: a pleasant, natural retreat on the surface, with a vague but palpable undercurrent of something wild and unpredictable, something scary and uncontrollable underneath. The kids' comedies were like that as much as the horror movies.

Wooden buildings formed a little village by the lake. Allison showed us an arts and crafts cabin with an outdoor stage facing a picnic-table pavilion, not far from a grassy field with a sports equipment shed. A dock extended into the water from a big shack of a boathouse stocked with colorful new canoes and kayaks.

"Have you experienced anything strange in this area?" I

asked.

"No, not here." She sighed. "I guess I'm just putting it off, but you should see it, if you're going to understand this place."

"Putting what off?"

"The Stony Owl, the place the camp is named after. The old native burial mound." She pointed toward the top of a high, densely wooded hill beyond the activity village. A steep trail wound up and around the hill, twisting out of sight among the trees. "I know it's a forgotten cultural treasure and all that, and I'm glad we're taking care of it, but... it's not a place I'd want to be alone."

A cold feeling crawled up my back at her words. Stacey looked at me, and I knew she felt something similar.

"We better go before it gets dark." Allison started up the trail, marked with another weather-worn sign: STONY OWL EFFIGY.

"You said it's a burial mound?" I asked, following close, making sure my flashlight was in its holster though we still had an hour of daylight left.

"That's what the archaeologist said, a hundred years ago or whenever anyone last tried to study it. They found bones under it, and lot of old artifacts."

The trail to the effigy hill skirted the lake and was muddy, slurping at my boots. An occasional short footbridge or fallen trunk offered passage over particularly sunken and wet areas. The canopy converged tightly above us, keeping the daylight scarce.

We began the steep path. It coiled up a high hill like a constrictor snake around its latest victim. There were points where I had to pull myself up with the nearby tree limbs.

"I know," Allison said, glancing back at my huffing and puffing. "We're almost there."

"I'm fine," I lied.

At last, the trail flattened out as promised. The trees were thinner at the top. Large chunks of overgrown stone were scattered alongside the trail, some of them waist-high.

"Was there a wall here?" I asked.

"That's what they think," Allison replied. "The ruins of old walls. Here we go."

Stepping through a gap in the wall ruins and the trees, we emerged into a clearing at the hilltop enclosed by an old chain-link fence. An immense pile of rocks stood there like a slag heap at a quarry, some portions of it as high as my shoulders, others eroded down into patches of weeds. All the weeds had been recently cut.

"We've been clearing it off," she said. "Josh thinks it's great we have such a significant historical site here, but like I said... working up here bothers me. Maybe it's just knowing this is a burial ground."

"Yeah, that can make a place pretty eerie," Stacey agreed.

"They think it was probably a chief or somebody like that. They obviously didn't build such a mound for just anyone. There are only a few in the whole state."

"Who built all this?" I asked.

She shrugged. "That's completely lost to history. We're talking about the Woodland Period, thousands of years ago. The observation tower's safe, if you want a good look."

We started toward a three-story concrete tower that reminded me of a lighthouse, narrow windows spaced around it in a spiral. A shiny new padlock held shut a heavy plank door. Allison unlocked it and pushed it open.

My stomach was knotting; the burial mound was getting to me. Nothing about the dim interior of the tower lifted my mood. Wide stairs twisted up and away, lit only by the windows; there was no electricity.

"You can't really see the owl from the ground," Allison said, leading the way up. "And it still takes a little imagination to see it from above, honestly."

I glanced back at Stacey as we ascended the steps. Her mood seemed to have dropped to match mine; she was no longer gushing about how much she liked the campground.

We walked around and around until we reached the viewing platform at the top. A railing overlooked the enormous rock effigy below.

"Oh, now I see it," Stacey said. "It looks like it's been nibbled around the edges, but yeah, I kinda see the horned owl shape."

From above, the heaps of stone were indeed roughly bird-shaped, the effigy's vast wings spread out as if in flight. As Stacey had mentioned, it was eroded around the edges, and only a few traces of its feet remained. The owl's head and horns had fared a bit better.

"It could just as well be a bat," I said.

"Well, everybody calls it Stony Owl, anyway," Allison said. "Who knows what it really is? We'd better get back. It's turning dark."

She started down, but I kept looking. The sun was sinking in the sky. From this hilltop tower, I had an expansive view of the forested mountains around us.

The sunset painted the owl with a reddish hue, and as the shadows shifted I could discern a pair of wide, shallow pits in the owl's head that must have represented its eyes. Perhaps time had largely erased them, drawing the sunken pits nearly level with the diminishing stone pile around it, or perhaps they'd been designed to be seen during certain times of the day when the sun's position cast shadows at the right angle. Like sunset, and maybe sunrise, too. When the sun was directly overhead at noon, the effigy might seem to have no eyes at all—as if its stony eyes closed for sleep during the day.

"Whatcha thinking about, Ellie?"

"Psychopomps," I said.

"Oh, yeah? Are those like... murderous cheerleaders?"

"There are old myths of birds guiding dead souls to the other side," I said. "Like ravens, or vultures, or owls. Sometimes carrion feeders. Sometimes nocturnal birds."

Stacey nodded. "And she said this was a grave. So they had an owl god, or something. Right?"

"Must have." As the sun crept lower, the great stony owl's eyes seemed to darken and to stare back up at me, perhaps regarding me as an intruder on its ancient, sacred land.

Chapter Six

"This is where my family is staying. I mean, it's where we live. I'm not fully adjusted to calling it 'home' yet." Allison showed the way ahead with her own flashlight; the night's gloom was creeping fast now. "The caretaker's cottage."

"That is one nice-sized cottage," Stacey said, taking in the patchwork house, made of a variety of different materials, as if it had been expanded piecemeal over the years. It sat back in the woods, its odd angles making it difficult to estimate how big it really was. A stone chimney rose from somewhere near the center of it.

"It's a maze inside, but there's plenty of room for the five of us." She walked past her black Lexus and up the steps to the cabin's covered porch. The old roof slanted low, like a dark hood over the house's face, casting the front door and windows into shadow, echoing the main lodge out on the opposite end of the campground. "I'll show you around before they get home."

The interior matched the exterior. The old floorboards were warped and slanted; if you'd set a ball on the floor at the front of the room, it would have rolled to the back. Two mismatched interior doors, different sizes and colors, led deeper into the house. There were built-in hooks and shelves for coats and shoes, a basic mud room.

Allison led us through one small, cluttered room after another, none of them matching, none of them particularly well-aligned with each other. We passed through a boxy room with a stone fireplace and a ladder up to a loft; she said this was the original cabin, to which more rooms had been affixed in every direction over the years.

While the house and fixtures were beyond rustic, the furniture was almost inappropriately nice, from the enormous dove-white leather couch and matching armchair crammed tightly in front of the fireplace to the mahogany cabinet full of delicate china, shoved out of the way down a short back hall where nobody could see it.

"The last straw for me happened here, in my room," Allison said.

We entered a startlingly large, new, fully modern bedroom with a king-size bed and a cavernous closet leading to a marble-accented bathroom. Picture windows looked out onto deep woods outside. The furniture here looked as nice the furniture elsewhere in the house, but not so awkwardly crammed into place; this room was large enough to accommodate their belongings.

"Josh built this whole master section for us. For me, really." She smiled a little. "The kids got original rooms and the original bathroom—well, new fixtures, of course—but all this is brand new. To give Josh and I little retreat. This is the kind of work he did back home. Luxury and comfort. Only the best."

"I can see," I said, gently dying of jealousy at the closet with its innumerable shelves and cabinets and drawers. I could really get my life organized with a closet like that. It was roughly the size of my apartment in Savannah. Maybe I could remake my whole apartment into a closet. A live-in closet. That could be a thing.

"So what did you experience in here?" Stacey asked, getting us back on course. Stacey was gazing out the huge windows into the dark woods the way I'd been gazing at the incredibly useful closet.

"It happened late one night," Allison said. "I couldn't sleep. Normally that's not hard after a day of work around here. Something was bothering me, though.

"I kept thinking about the big owl and the bones they found under it. It's like having a graveyard right there, up on the hill behind our house. Most of the time I don't think about it, but that night I couldn't keep my mind off it. I wondered who was buried there, and how many people. It's hard to say why it was on my mind so much. Josh was snoring louder than usual, so that didn't help.

"It was a little after two in the morning when I heard the footsteps. They reminded me of what I'd heard up at the main lodge, but I'd never heard them way back here at the cabin before.

"I lay there, wide awake, listening. The footsteps sounded like they were right outside, like someone was in the yard.

"Those picture windows made me feel dangerously exposed. They were just too big, somebody could come smashing through them. The curtains were closed, so I couldn't see what was happening out there.

"The footsteps came right up to that window." Allison indicated one that looked out onto the wooded hillside that led up to Stony Owl. "Then they stopped. I froze up, waiting for more...waiting for the other shoe to fall, I guess. Nothing happened.

"After a minute, I figured the only way to settle my mind would be to get up and take a peek out through the curtains. Once I saw nothing was outside, I'd be able to relax. That was the idea.

"It was strange how hard it was to push myself out of bed, to take those steps to the window. Like my legs were reluctant to go. The closer I got to the curtain, the more I was sure I'd see something horrible when I looked out.

"I forced myself to reach up and take hold of the curtain's edge. I told myself I'd just pull it open enough to peek out, to see there was nothing out there. Maybe some wildlife.

"There was a little moonlight, so when I pulled open the curtain, jut wide enough I could see the trees up along the hill. There's a break in the woods, and an overgrown path that leads up the hill and connects with the main trail. At first I thought something might have wandered out from the old path, maybe a bear.

"What I saw out there was no animal, though. It was a shadow in the moonlight, right outside the window, shaped like a person but taller than any person really could be.

"I let go of the curtain, and it fell back into place so I couldn't see the shadow anymore. I tried to call out to Josh, but my throat was all closed up. I couldn't even back away from the window, even though I kept telling my legs to move. It was like I was nailed into place.

"So I stood there, staring at the curtain, being totally useless.

"Then I heard them again: the footsteps, right in front of me, just beyond that big, fragile pane of glass. They moved that way." Allison turned, pointing to the next window. "They stopped there. Then that curtain bulged out. The glass didn't break or anything; it was like the glass wasn't there at all, like our window was wide open and something big was coming through it.

"I thought I would die of fright right there. You'd think I would have been able to yell for my husband, but instead it was like one of those nightmares where you can't move, where you're trapped in place.

"The curtain bulged out and out. When it dropped back into place, the tall shadow figure was in the room with me. I couldn't tell if he was looking at me, or getting ready to attack me, or what he would do. I was terrified he would speak. I couldn't imagine what might happen if he came toward me. None of it made sense—how could he have gotten inside like that?

"He walked across my room, and I thought he was coming toward me at first. He went right past me, though. Then I worried he was walking toward Josh, but he kept on moving, out the door and into the hall.

"Before it walked out of sight, I noticed it was holding something in its hand, something long and narrow, a stick or a knife, I don't know. It was only a shadow, like I said, and it was gone almost the moment I noticed it.

"When the shadow was out of sight down the hall, my feet finally came unstuck from the floor. Suddenly I could speak again, and I started yelling Josh's name.

"I ran after the shadow, because it was heading toward the kids' rooms. I don't know what I thought I'd do if I caught up to it, but I was out in the hall before Josh was even out of bed.

"I turned on the hall light, but I didn't see anything." Allison pointed up the crooked, tightly turning hallway. "I checked on each of the kids. They were mostly fine; my yelling stirred them up. Except Shiloh. She was sitting up in her bed like she'd been wide awake for a while. But she didn't say anything, and she wasn't hurt. Just playing with her dolls and humming to herself.

"There was nobody in the house. The shadow-man vanished like smoke. I looked around without explaining what I was looking for, because I knew it would sound crazy. I made sure the doors were locked, the windows were latched. Then I told the kids there was nothing to worry about and I'd just had a bad dream.

"Later, I told Josh what really happened, and he bought into the story I'd made up for the kids. He insisted it had to be a dream. But like I said, I was already wide awake before any of it happened. Finally, I told Josh—*enough*. Something unnatural is happening around here, and we're going to get some help or else we are leaving. That's what I said. Ultimatum time. Maybe my mind played tricks once or twice, but not that many times, okay? I am not crazy." Her mouth pressed into a tight, angry line.

"I understand," I said. "It sounds like you've had some intense experiences here."

She nodded, seeming a little relieved that I hadn't called her crazy. "So what do you think? In your professional opinion?"

"I usually collect more information before forming an

opinion," I said. "We typically set up an overnight observation and try to detect any evidence of an entity. That might be as subtle as a cold spot or electromagnetic disturbance, or as obvious as the apparition you described. In your case, this would include cameras and microphones in your room; you and your husband might stay in another room during the investigation. We would also set up around the lodge where you heard the footsteps, and the cabin with the possible disturbance where the tools were knocked around, and where your daughter reports seeing people."

"Honestly, I'm not sure about that part," Allison said. "Shy is always making things up. She had imaginary friends back home, too. La-La the Lollipop Lizard. Bucko the Talking Slime Bucket. A lot of others. She doesn't pay attention in school, gets in trouble for drawing pictures all over her worksheets."

"Still, I'd like to hear what she has to say, if it's okay with you. Young children are often more sensitive to the paranormal."

"Maybe tomorrow." Allison checked the time on her phone. "They should be back in a few minutes, and I'll barely have a chance to feed them before Shy's bedtime. I don't want to get her all stirred up about this tonight."

"It will take a while to set up our gear," I said. "We could get started now."

"I'm not sure we're ready to have all that in our home," Allison said. "I'd like to do it, of course. But I'll need to talk it over with Josh, then explain to the kids. What about the main lodge? Could you start there tonight? And maybe start on this house tomorrow?"

"We definitely could." My next question was awkward but felt necessary. "Is your family aware we're here? And why?"

"I told Josh about it, but not the kids. And he's not necessarily expecting you to stay here and get to work right away. So, yes, there is plenty to discuss. But I'm not letting this go until we figure out what's happening."

Allison drove us back to our van. Stacey sat in the back seat, thumbing through a Mo Willems Pig and Elephant picture book she'd found on the car seat. The drive took a minute along a narrow dirt road around the outer edge of the camp to reach the lodge parking lot.

"We'll update you in the morning," I told Allison, just before I hopped out. "I wouldn't expect too much on the first night, especially since we're starting small. But hopefully we can shed some light on whatever's been troubling you."

"A flashlight, at least," Stacey said, grinning a little as she stepped out. "Or even an itsy-bitsy little pen light."

"Good luck. And stay safe." Allison frowned at the dark old lodge looming over us before driving away.

"I don't know if this place is haunted, but it's definitely creepy," Stacey said. "It's hard to imagine kids enjoying it. Except maybe those nicer cabins. And that arts and crafts spot looked cool. Maybe the lake, too."

"If it's haunted, kids will be sensitive to that."

"Which will kinda ruin camp for them. Or make it extra cool?"

"If there's a dangerous entity involved, it would not be cool."

"True," Stacey said. "Kids do hate getting stalked and murdered in the woods."

"Let's get to work." I opened the side door on the old cargo van. "We may finally get to put some of your camping skills to use, Stacey."

"Yes!" she exclaimed, but she was faking her enthusiasm. Her eyes drifted to the shadowy lodge where we'd be spending the night, and her attempted smile collapsed. Her worried frown mirrored the expression Allison had worn while hurriedly driving away.

Chapter Seven

"Well, isn't that super cheerful?" Stacey asked, shaking her head.

The dead horned owl perched inside a Plexiglas cube on a pedestal in the lodge's little museum. It had been preserved decades earlier and was crumbling with time, shedding many of its feathers into a dry drift like a heap of fallen leaves at the bottom of the cube. Its yellow glass eyes seemed to glare at us with disdain.

"Are owls always that big?" I asked. The owl stood three feet tall, from the hornlike tufts on its head down to its talons, which were nailed to its crumbling tree-branch perch.

"No, he's a monster specimen," Stacey said. "I feel bad for the poor owl. Stuck in that box forever like some dead Russian dictator."

"One more thing to get rid of before any kids arrive

for camp, if you ask me," I said.

The museum wasn't large, but there was a lot packed into it, all displayed behind Plexiglas cabinet doors. One side focused on the minerals, plants, and wildlife of the Chattahoochee National Forest where the campground was located.

The other focused on human history, featuring assorted artifacts and sepia-toned pictures of the amateur archaeologist who'd unearthed them.

There were pictures of the great stone owl as it had been discovered in the 1800s, thick with weeds and thorns, its full shape unknown until the hostile vegetation had been cut away. More pictures gave examples of the crumbling remnants of the old stone wall that had lined the spiraling path in ancient days.

"So, that whole burial ground thing, I see major redness, flag-wise," Stacey said. "Am I right?"

"Potentially." I approached a glass display case full of pottery shards. Alongside these were an obsidian knife and a stone ax head. Another shelf held decorative items—a sheet of copper not much larger than a sheet of notebook paper. An owl was etched into it with outstretched wings like the effigy outside. There was a small circle of silver etched with what could have been a beaver or badger. At the bottom of the case, a handful of quartzite stones taken from the effigy on the hill were arranged in the shape of a tiny owl, imitating the shape of the real one.

"Little is known about the mysterious builders of Stony Owl," Stacey read from the display, in a sort of over-the-top lecturing tone, like she'd always been the world's greatest expert on this particular site. "They were believed to be hunter-gatherers of the Woodland Period between

1000 BC and 1000 AD. Grave items indicate ancient continental trade networks—silver from the Great Lakes area, shells from the Gulf Coast, obsidian from the Yellowstone region."

I looked at the old pictures of the excavation, dated 1896. The archaeologist, an old white man with a straw hat and a lengthy beard, knelt in front of a trench dug into the stony owl. He held a handful of decorative beads in one hand.

In his other hand, held up like a gruesome trophy, was a human skull.

"Yikes." I shivered. "I hope they put that back where they found it."

"Looks like they kept some of it." Stacey pointed to the beads in the display. They were carved from yellowed bone and decayed bits of wood. "That could stir up the ghosts, right?"

"Maybe. Though with artifacts this old, most of the entities associated with them should have moved on long ago. I would hope so. Thousand-year-old entities are rare, but they're always unnerving. And dangerous. They've long since lost touch with their brief existence as a living thing." I shook my head. "Anyway, let's not jump to conclusions. This isn't even the area where she heard footsteps."

Further exploration of the museum turned up no skeletal remains from the dig, fortunately.

There was an area devoted to the camp's founder, a tall, broad-shouldered, stern-looking preacher by the name of Roger Carmody; his plump wife Laurie Ann stood beside him, smiling wide as if to make up for his solemn expression. They wore uniforms and wide-brimmed campaign hats like park rangers or state troopers. So did all the young campers. *"Discipline, industry, and loyalty are the building blocks of character,"* said one of several quotes pasted around Carmody's oversized black and white picture, in which he addressed precise rows of uniformed boys and girls.

We left a lone night vision camera watching the museum. Allison hadn't reported trouble there, but a room full of excavated grave goods was worth keeping an eye on.

In the office, we pointed our cameras and microphones toward the windows, which we left open. If anything walked by in the night, hopefully we'd catch evidence of it.

"Well, that just leaves the attic." Stacey was leaning against Allison's desk, looking up at the somewhat saggy ceiling. "She didn't mention what was up there, did she?"

"She did not. Other than footsteps and strange sounds." I couldn't help feeling apprehensive. The set-up had taken awhile, and it was completely dark outside. Very little silvery moonlight fell through the clouds to illuminate the night. I could barely make out the edges of the thick porch post outside the window.

We had to poke around for a minute to even find the attic stairs. They were at the back of a narrow closet with a mop bucket and broom, hidden behind a dusty louvered door that emitted a scratchy rasp as I opened it.

The only illumination over the stairs was a bare bulb on a string; we added our flashlights to that. The stairs felt like a rickety afterthought, wooden slats with no risers between them, just gaps looking into musty darkness.

The second floor had a definite forgotten-attic feel, ceiling low and slanted, bare rafters close enough to touch. Most of the space was cluttered with memories of summers past—broken oars, baseball bats, a broken heap of an old tent shoved into one corner. One box overflowed with grimy old trophies from long-forgotten events.

"Now that is... really unusual." I pointed with my flashlight, but Stacey was already looking.

A structure resembling one of the camper cabins outside had been built here in the attic, taking up the back quarter of the space. It had a door with a keyhole lock, and even had small windows looking out onto the attic. Nearby, iron pots and a kettle hung by the fireplace.

"For when you want to camp out, but not really, I guess," Stacey said

"Kind of eccentric."

Unlike the downstairs, the upstairs had only a few small windows; it would be dim even in daytime.

We moved aside a lumpy, hand-carved wooden wagon, a couple of deflated balls, and some assorted toy soldiers and rag dolls, making room for camera tripods and recorders. While Stacey set up those, I poked around some more.

The floorboards creaked heavily as I approached the odd indoor cabin in the corner. The whole structure gave me an uneasy feeling.

I turned the knob. The door opened reluctantly, as if it had been stuck shut for many years.

Inside was an old bedroom, an austere, spartan space, the bed barely a double. Two small, plain wardrobes occupied the corners. A desk faced the room's single small window. There was a small, dark bathroom in the corner, the door ajar.

The little attic cabin had been claimed for storage over the years, crates and boxes shoved in haphazardly, piled up on the floor and almost burying the furniture. Everything smelled profoundly musty.

"I think I found the old headmaster's quarters," I told Stacey. "Or whatever you call the head of a camp. Warden?"

"Director. Warden is for prisons."

"Yeah, I don't know why I'd think of this spooky, cramped old place as a prison. How are we here?"

"All set, I think. I threw in a couple of motion detectors," Stacey said.

"Good." I looked over the array of gear and nodded, then started for the stairs. "Let's get out of the way and see what happens."

We tiptoed downstairs and out the front door, then climbed into the back of the van. We'd use it as our nerve center, watching the array of little monitors and listening to the speakers. We were using fewer than half the available screens.

"I'm wiped out," I said, sitting back to watch and listen. "I'm glad we only did one building tonight."

"It's going to be hard to monitor so many sites spread out like that," Stacey said.

"Good thing that's tomorrow night's problem." I cracked open an absurdly tall can of something that claimed to be green tea under layers of added sugar and caffeine. I looked from the night vision view of the museum, to the cluttered attic, to the first-floor area around the office. "Seems like pretty decent coverage for a quick job."

"Not that quick. It's almost eleven," Stacey said.

"Really? Feels later."

We fell quiet, watching and listening. The van sat in the desolate parking lot, the only vehicle there. I tried not to think about how isolated the campground was, or to imagine anyone emerging from the thick woods around us.

Something had inflicted the damage to the lodge and to Bobcat Cabin, after all; human or beast, alive or dead.

We kept the van's doors locked. I double-checked a couple of times to make sure.

Chapter Eight

Despite our surroundings, and the discomfort of my drop-down cot in the van, I dozed off at some point. So, it turned out, did Stacey.

While I realize that literally sleeping on the job might not sound super-professional on our part, it had been a five-hour drive involving hair-raising, adrenaline-extracting steep mountain roads overlooking steep mountain drops to steep mountain deaths. Then we'd spent hours with the client and setting up cameras and such.

The microphones in the office caught the night sounds of the mountain forest through the open windows—fluttering wings of unseen birds and bats, frogs croaking from the lake and creeks. Scrabbling, scratching, screeching. A coyote howled. Owls did some weird cackling cries that sounded like a troop of monkeys threatening each other in the trees.

All of this became a constant background, calming in its way. Even in the uncomfortable van, it had been easy to grow accustomed to the night sounds and doze off.

I awoke to a sudden, sharp cry.

"What was that?" I asked. "Stacey, are you okay?"

In the gray glow of the monitor screens, Stacey was on her cot, solidly zonked out. I could wake her, but she wouldn't be able to tell me what I'd heard.

Something moved at the corner of my eye. A flicker on a monitor, but I wasn't sure which one.

I crept toward the monitors, looking intently from one to the other, listening carefully.

There.

Something moved in the monochrome image from a night vision camera up in the lodge's attic.

It was barely noticeable. The little hand-carved wagon, one of the toys we'd slid aside to clear our path, was nose first against a table leg. I'd glimpsed it shifting backward less than a centimeter, a movement so slight it could almost have been my imagination.

It wasn't, though. I grabbed Stacey's laptop and pulled up the recording of that camera's footage.

When I replayed the recent footage, it didn't take long to find what I was looking for.

The little toy wagon—it really was crude, handmade, a seemingly careless creation from a half-attempted craft activity in the distant past—wobbled forward on its uneven wheels as if pushed by an unseen hand. It moved through the legs of the thermal camera's tripod and back to where we'd originally found it, a distance of several inches.

It bumped into the table leg, then rocked back a little before stopping. That was the small movement I'd initially seen.

"Stacey!" I said, louder than before, while I played the footage in reverse.

"Huh?" Stacey looked toward me with sleepy eyes, her blond hair sticking up high on one side, staticky bedhead creating a punk look. "Whatsa?"

"Look at this."

While she came over, rubbing her eyes, I noticed something else a minute earlier in the footage than the inexplicably moving wagon. A long-deflated red rubber ball shifted on the floor, as if someone had tried to roll it. It didn't go far, just twitched like a dying blobfish and fell still again.

"Whoa," Stacey said, leaning forward and tuning in to the situation. "Some real psychokinetic activity in there."

"Check the upstairs audio recording for spikes," I said, continuing to work at the laptop.

"Got it." Stacey grabbed a tablet.

"The EMF meter went wild for a minute there," I told her as I checked through the data. "A temperature drop, like an entity came through. We should have caught something on thermal."

Stacey made a slight *mmph* sound, like maybe she was listening, maybe not. "There *was* an audio spike," she said, looking at the digital graph of soundwaves. "Let's have us a listen, shall we?"

She played the audio. As the vertical tracking line crossed the sharp peak, a high shriek filled the van. We jumped, even though we'd been expecting something. The audio returned to normal after that. We hadn't opened any upstairs windows, so the attic was fairly silent, aside from the occasional creaking of the lodge's old timbers or the occasional especially loud owl.

I looked at the live feed from the cameras upstairs. At the moment, nothing moved on the night vision camera. The thermal showed a leaky draft around the small window, but no particularly cold spots.

"Something passed through, anyway," I said. "What did that sound like to you?"

"A scream, maybe?" Stacey played it again—it was high-pitched, abrupt, and brief. "It's only about a quarter-second long. Like something you might overhear from a passing car. Could be a scared scream or happy scream. Maybe even a really painful laugh."

"Anything on the thermal?"

"Playing it backwards at quarter speed." Stacey watched her screen. I kept my eyes on the live monitors, but nothing else seemed to be happening.

After a minute, Stacey spoke up again, oddly quiet and serious: "Ellie?"

"What?"

She turned the screen toward me and played some of the thermal video.

For a period of several seconds, the thermal showed a cold blue mist filling the attic. It was like a burst of volcanic eruptions or geysers, only icy instead of hot.

The cold grew and grew, enveloping most of the room. Stacey paused the video.

"That's... kinda big, isn't it?" Stacey asked, her voice hushed.

"Yeah. That's really quite a presence." I didn't know what else to say; I just stared.

We'd certainly detected cold spots before, but there was something different here. Usually they were concentrated in one place, sometimes taking on the rough shape of human beings, sometimes not.

I wasn't sure what to make of the cloud of cold that had passed through the room. It was huge, swelling to fill much of the attic before shrinking away and vanishing.

Stacey played it back more slowly. I shook my head.

"That's weird," I said. An understatement.

"It's enormous. I hope we don't get on its bad side. Whichever side that may be." She frowned at the shapeless presence.

As I watched the vast coldness flowing through the cluttered attic, it was like I could feel it right through the recorded video, the chill eating through my skin and down into my bones.

"What do you think it is?" Stacey whispered.

"I don't know," I said. "It makes me think of vampire stories."

"I thought they turned into bats."

"Bats, wolves, mist. The really top-notch ones turn into all three."

"So you think it's a vampire? Like from Sookie Stackhouse?"

"I doubt it. Myths and folklore tend to be rooted in truth, though." I looked over at the live feed from the thermal video, but there was nothing happening in real time. The enormous cold presence had filled the attic and vanished in a matter of seconds, as though just passing through on its way from the afterworld, leaving us with lots of questions and no answers at all.

Chapter Nine

I remained wide awake for the rest of the night; having watched some giant presence pass through the lodge's upper floor, nudging objects, I was eager to see whether it came back or not.

After a few hours, I was even tempted to head in there with a voice recorder and ask a few questions, try to elicit a response from the entity, but I didn't want to rush into anything the first night. I forced myself to be patient and observe.

In the last darkness before sunrise, unexpected bright lights filled the front of the van. From where we sat in the back, looking at the monitors built in behind the driver and shotgun seats, we couldn't see the source of the light.

"Allison must be coming to check on us." I looked at my phone to see if I'd missed a text or call from her, but I hadn't.

The lights held steady, like a police car studying a potential suspect. I clambered over to the driver's seat and looked out. I couldn't see much but the headlights.

Being in an annoyed, sleep-deprived kind of mood, I kicked open the driver door and hopped out. My hand lingered against the tactical flashlight holstered at my belt, which can make a handy weapon when needed.

"Can I help you?" I asked, stepping out of the beams so I could see better. It was a Jaguar sedan that looked out of place at the campground. Its low-slung chassis was thoroughly painted in mud. It was parked sloppily, across two spaces, but I guess there wasn't much demand for parking at the moment.

I approached the tinted window and knocked.

The glass rolled down. The guy behind it was in his forties, with a deep tan, close-cropped blond hair, and a toothy grin. I had the impression he was about to invite me to watch a video about timeshare condos, which was similar to the impression I'd gotten from his picture on his wife's desk.

"Hey there." He reached out a hand for me to shake. His grip was firm, and his eyes sparkled as he looked at me, as though he were laughing inwardly at some joke, possibly at my expense. "Josh Conner. Nice to meet you. I thought I'd swing by and try to understand what's happening up here."

I introduced myself. "I'm sure your wife told you why we're here."

"She did, yes. To be honest, I thought she was joking." He killed his lights and engine and stepped out, towering over me, a few inches past six feet. He was a guy who kept in shape. He wore a faded linen shirt and designer jeans, and he flashed me a sale-closing smile, his teeth movie-star white. "Then last night she mentioned you were actually here."

"We actually are, yes." I introduced Stacey as she came around to join us.

"Do you do ghost tours?" he asked.

"I'm sorry?"

"She said you're paranormal investigators from Savannah. We went on a ghost tour there once. A haunted trolley ride at night. Well, a bus, but they call it a trolley. They told us about all the haunted places downtown."

"Most of the places downtown are haunted or allegedly haunted," I said. "But no, we are not on the tourism side of things."

"We enjoyed it. Lovely city, very inspirational. Our Heritage Green development in Alpharetta was meant to look like a square lifted from Savannah. Those units sold fast. I can show you pictures."

"Sounds nice," I said, hoping he didn't mean right away, or maybe ever.

"Allison said you were planning to spend the night in the lodge," he said. "What did you think?"

"Well, we actually—"

"I know it still needs work, but we're hoping to build on the history here. We want arcs of connection between today and yesterday, a tapestry of many traditions. The old days of the camp, its past eras, and of course the native people who lived here in ancient times. We want to honor the past while looking ahead to the future."

"It sounds like you're ready to start selling the place to parents," I said.

Josh chuckled. "We've already been at it. Nineteen

campers are reserved for our opening week in June."

"You think you'll be ready by then?" My eyebrows climbed skyward.

"We'd better be! Who wants the ten-cent tour?"

"I think your wife gave us that yesterday."

"Did she show you the dining hall? I could whip up some waffles. We've got the latest in waffle irons."

I glanced at Stacey, who nodded vigorously.

"Good. That'll give me an excuse to make one for myself." He led us past the main lodge to the dining hall, low and long, mostly hidden in the woods, its wall made of enormous logs.

A wooden porch of a loading dock faced the parking lot; Josh unlocked one of the double doors and led us into a sizable kitchen, most of it shiny and new, some appliances still wrapped in thick plastic.

"How do you like your waffles?" He took a bag of mixture from the cabinet and unclamped it. He looked at Stacey a moment, then said: "Let me guess—blueberry waffle. Topped with honey."

"Sounds great." She nodded sagely, as though she'd carefully weighed his proposition and found it reasonable.

Josh looked at me, then nodded. "Raspberries."

"Why?" I asked.

"They're straightforward. No nonsense."

"And blueberries are what? High nonsense?" Stacey asked.

"They do have that Violet Beauregard reputation," he replied. "But blueberries can be sensible, too."

"They're high in antioxidants."

"Good example." He was already at work, adding fresh berries before spooning the goopy white mixture onto the hot waffle iron. He was eager to describe the waffle iron's many advanced and unique properties to Stacey, who was either genuinely interested or too polite to act otherwise.

I drifted out of the kitchen, past the serving counter to the dining area. It had the same feel as the lodge, old hardwood floors and narrow windows and exposed rafters. CAMP STONY OWL was painted on the wall above a giant aerial photograph of the owl effigy.

The long tables and benches didn't look comfy, but they could seat dozens of muddy campers and just pretty much get hosed off afterward.

The windows were open, letting the cold morning breeze pass through, probably trying to erase the musty shut-in odor. The early daylight was lightening up the dark blue sky. A scattering of birds whistled and cawed at the breaking day, though it didn't seem like many considering we were surrounded by forest. A shivering squirrel climbed nervously along a limb outside, keeping a wary eye on me.

"Chow time, campers!" Josh announced. He carried a tray with two plates of waffles, one featuring blueberries and the other with raspberries. He set them out on the table along with forks rolled in napkins. "I offered coffee, but Stacey said y'all wouldn't want any."

"No, thanks, we've been up all—"

"I don't touch it anymore, either. Too many days of guzzling the stuff all morning, then wondering why I couldn't sleep at night. Swore it off a couple years ago. Now I jog in the morning—same wake-up jolt, but in a healthier way."

"That's smart." Stacey arrived with thick plastic cups and a carafe of orange juice.

"Thanks, Mr. Conner," I said. "This all looks great—"

"Hey, call me Josh, you're making me feel old here. I'm not going gray yet. Am I?" He touched his carefully arranged blond hair.

"Sorry, I didn't mean—"

"I'll be back in a flash." He returned to the kitchen while Stacey and I started in on our waffles. They were tasty, as various forms of sugary fried bread dough tend to be, and I was suddenly hungry.

"Who wants a little waffle booster?" Josh returned holding a can of whipped cream. Stacey volunteered.

"None for me," I said.

"I knew you were the no-nonsense one." He added cream to Stacey's waffle, then sat down to eat his own breakfast, a bowl of what looked like dried oats and twigs. "Which makes me wonder how you ended up doing this kind of thing."

"You mean the paranormal work?" I asked.

"Exactly. Ghost hunting. What's it all about?"

"Sometimes people have problems with the supernatural, or suspect they might. We help them figure it out."

"And how do you do that?" He took a spoonful of oats and sticks. They crunched loudly, painful to hear.

"It depends on the case. Our most important tool is knowledge. If we know why an entity is present, we can help it move on."

"And what exactly do you think is present here?" Josh was smiling when he spoke, but his eyes seemed a little hard, like he was examining me under the pretense of casual friendliness. I've probably worn that look myself, questioning witnesses to try to draw information out of them.

"We don't know just yet," I said. "Allison told us she's heard things around the main lodge and seen things in the caretaker's cottage where you live. Have you experienced anything abnormal since moving out here?"

"I sure have," he said. "I've seen my sons hammering and sanding and painting instead of drooling over their phones. I've seen more than a hundred different kinds of birds. I've seen the sunrise and the sunset every day, and not through a windshield while commuting."

"Yeah, it's pretty great out here," Stacey said, as if she didn't find the place spooky at all.

"Have you observed anything similar to what your wife described?" I pressed on, not getting distracted by his inspirational-poster description of things. "Strange footsteps? Shadowy figures?"

"White sheets with eyeholes floating around?" he asked. "Little green men? Bigfoot? No, I haven't seen anything like that. My wife wanted to have paranormal investigators come, she found you, I wasn't going to argue. Whatever sets her mind at ease. I just don't want to scare the kids. That's my main concern."

"I understand your daughter reports seeing people around the campground," I said. "People nobody else can see."

He laughed. "That's just Shy. She's always making things up."

"Do you think your wife is making things up, too?"

His easy smile tamped down slightly. "I didn't say that. Look, this is an unusual place for her. For all of us. We're accustomed to the city life. Being out here in the wild is an adjustment. It's easy to get scared in a strange place."

To me, that sounded like the long way of saying he

didn't really believe her.

"What about your other kids, the older ones? Has either of them seen anything?" I asked.

"The boys?" He was barely smiling now. "How's your waffle?"

"Good," I said, leaning back a little, like my stomach had grown too big to keep under the table any longer. "Amazingly good."

"So how much longer do you suppose all of this will take?" He gestured between Stacey and me. "This whole haunted house caper?"

"It's hard to predict. It could take several days to collect data and determine a possible course of action—"

"Days?" he asked. "Several *days?*"

"That would be typical."

"I thought you'd be out of here sometime today," he said. His big smile was back.

I wasn't sure how to respond, so I picked my words carefully. "We are only at the beginning. We haven't even tried to collect data from your family's house, where your wife saw the big shadow figure. We certainly haven't resolved the situation."

"So you're planning to stick around awhile."

"That's up to you and your wife," I said. "If y'all want us to keep investigating, that's what we're looking at."

"Sounds expensive."

"Room and board can get pricey on these out of town cases."

"But he's got waffles," Stacey said, before forking up the last bite of hers. "I'll work for waffles."

"Josh?" Allison emerged from the kitchen area. "I thought you were down in boy town."

"I will be. You want a waffle? Or some Stoneground Oaters?" He gestured at his cereal with a spoon.

"I'd rather not break my teeth." She grimaced at his cereal. "Anybody else want coffee?" We all shook our heads, and Allison sighed before going to the giant steel urn behind the counter. "How did it go last night?" she asked over her shoulder.

"We collected some very compelling data," I replied.

"You didn't mention that," Josh said.

"We were much too dazzled by the waffle iron and all that it created," Stacey said.

"Oh, Josh is very happy with that waffle iron," Allison said.

"Stacey will bring in her computer to show you as soon as she's done with her waffle," I said.

"But I'm already done with my—oh, okay." Stacey headed for the door.

By the time she was back, Allison had swept by to clear away our dishes.

"They say they're planning to stay for *days*," Josh said. "We have to pay their hotel fees."

"Or we could camp!" Stacey suggested, because of course she did.

"You're welcome to stay in one of the girls' cabins," Allison said. "They're ready to go."

"Sounds awesome!" Stacey said. "They are really pretty —"

"We should stay on the boys' side," I interrupted. "It sounds like there's possible activity over there."

Stacey and Allison both winced at this idea.

"You bet! I'd recommend Wolf or Falcon Cabin. Definitely not Bobcat or Warthog." Josh chuckled. "Not unless you're *really* into roughing it." He eyeballed Stacey's laptop suspiciously as she pulled up files.

"So here's what we found." I pointed at the thermal camera footage. "Over a period of thirty-three seconds, this cold spot appeared, filled the attic, then shrank away again."

"Well, we know the lodge gets cold," Josh said.

"We also caught two objects moving without any clear reason."

The video showed the rolling wagon, then the old ball shifting a little.

Allison took in a sharp breath. "This is right over the office, isn't it?" she asked.

I nodded.

"The floors in this place are all warped." Josh said. "Round things roll. We need to be rational about this."

"Sure," Allison said. "And the noises I've been hearing up there for weeks? And the thing in our room? Is that all just me being irrational, Josh?"

"Hey, sorry." Josh held up his hands in mock surrender. "You got me."

"You said you would support me on this," Allison said.

"I'm supporting, I'm supporting. I'm just worried about scaring the kids. Should we tell them these ladies are here to make a promotional video for the camp? That will explain all the cameras."

"Though probably not why there's one in our bedroom," Allison said.

"Just set that one up while we're all away at the cabin site." Josh nodded like he was confirming this to himself. "Yep. That'll work."

"What do you think?" Allison asked me.

"I was actually hoping to ask your kids if they'd seen anything," I said.

"Ephraim might have," Allison said. "He keeps telling me he thinks the whole campground is eerie—"

"Ephraim was a complainer before we got here," Josh said. "Nate hasn't complained at all. He likes it here."

"If Ephraim said the sky was blue, Nate would say it was red," Allison said. "Nate's just not as sensitive as Ephraim."

"Nate's a go-getter. A hard worker. We need more Nateness around here, if you ask me, and a little less Ephraimity," Josh said. "So is that all? The attic's cold? Something moved up there? What does that prove?"

"We also recorded a voice." I nodded at Stacey to play it.

Allison stared at the soundwave graph on the screen as the high-pitched shriek sounded from the speakers.

"That's not—" Josh began.

"Play it again," Allison said.

Stacey did, the odd shriek filling the room again. And again.

"That could be a bird," Josh said.

"It is not a bird. I'm tired of you telling me it's my imagination. I'm tired of trying to tell *myself* that. I am not crazy." Allison's voice hadn't risen too much, but her eyes smoldered like they were about to burn holes into Josh's face.

"Okay, hey, I never implied you were crazy," Josh said. "We're having it investigated. They're here. Right? I want to put you at ease about this."

"Which, again, makes me sound crazy."

"I didn't mean—"

"Forget it." Allison looked at us. "We're moving ahead with this investigation. Feel free to do whatever you have to do."

"Just give us a chance to keep the kids out of the way," Josh added, and I nodded.

After breakfast, Allison went back to rejoin the kids. Josh helped us carry our belongings from the van to our assigned cabin on the boys' side—Wolf Cabin, identified by the furry predator painted by the door, updated by Allison with sunglasses and a toothy Big Bad Wolf grin.

"I really think you'd be happier in one of the girls' cabins," Josh said as he led us inside.

Wolf Cabin was definitely rougher than the cheerful dollhouse interiors over at the girls' area, with none of the bright colors. Dark wooden walls and metal bunk beds, four beds to a room, no ceiling fan. Thankfully, the bedding looked new, as did the plumbing in the three-stall bathroom. The furniture in the common area, not so much.

"At least you've got it all to yourselves, for what that's worth," Josh said.

"This will be fine," I said. "Thank you."

"Can we make a fire?" Stacey pointed out a window to the fire ring outside. "I mean, not right now, but at some point."

"Have you earned your fire safety badge?" Josh asked her.

"Pfft, you should see my old Camp Mizpah award sash. It's heavy with survival skills bling."

"I doubt we'll need a campfire," I said, drawing a scathing look from Stacey. "Thanks again, Josh."

"Call us if you need anything. Or text Allison. She seems pretty happy to have you here, so I hope you can make her feel better about... whatever all this is."

"We'll do what we can."

"In fact," he said, "I could toss in a bonus. The faster you make her feel better—the sooner you convince her there's nothing to be scared of here—the bigger that could be. You see what I mean?"

"Um," I said, as Stacey gaped at him. "Sure. I'll think about that."

"Great! I understand you need to make a living. I just don't want you to think you'll get more money by dragging things out."

"We have no intention of—"

"I know, I know! I think we all understand each other. You'll do better by speeding it along and telling her we're fine here. Now rest up. I know you've got a big night of ghost busting ahead, right?"

He beamed another smile at me before heading out, leaving Stacey and me there in Wolf Cabin.

Chapter Ten

After Josh left, Stacey and I sat on bunk beds and looked at each other.

"Did he just... try to bribe us into saying the place isn't haunted?" Stacey asked.

"That's what it sounded like to me," I agreed. "He doesn't believe it, he thinks we're here for his wife's peace of mind. But obviously we're not taking his offer."

"Obviously! I couldn't believe he said that. How dishonest."

"He probably thinks he can create a placebo effect. He doesn't think there's a real problem, and he clearly suspects we're scam artists, but he's willing to pay us off anyway if we can put Allison's fears to rest."

"It sounds like you're defending him."

"I'm not. Just trying to understand our situation. Sometimes not everybody in the family is on board with a paranormal investigation, but this might be the first time somebody wanted me to lie to the rest of the family. I think he's trying to protect them in his own way; he thinks the real danger is Allison spreading panic around."

"Well, I still don't approve of his dishonesty." Stacey unzipped her backpack full of clothes and overnight supplies.

"Do you want to hit the showers with me?" I asked. "I'm covered in three layers of road grit, and I'm not going to that bathhouse alone."

"Sure."

The boys' showers were extremely non-glamorous, with lots of exposed concrete and brick. I wore some cheap flip-flops I'd brought in case of motel showers. Campground showers were a notch or two below that, or at least this one was.

The bathhouse, like the rest of the campground, had an eerie feeling. The place had once been thronged with kids and teenagers, loud, busy. It was silent, yet somehow invisibly populated with hidden memories of years past.

This feeling of unseen presences made me hurry through my shower, though I still ended up waiting for Stacey, who took her time, singing her childhood camp song.

Back at Wolf Cabin, Stacey lay back on the bunk and closed her eyes. "This is not super comfortable," she mumbled, her last words before falling asleep.

Tired but restless, I got up and explored the cabin. There wasn't much to it—the shabby common room where we'd entered, two bedrooms, a bathroom with a couple of stalls but no tub or shower. There was a smaller room with a sink and single bed where the resident counselor would one day sleep.

Through the windows, I surveyed the cabins, including the dilapidated Bobcat Cabin, the one where the night visitor had knocked Josh's tools around.

I tried to relax by sitting at the wobbly coffee table in the common room, looking over my notes and typing them up in a more formal way in a computer file, filling in our usual template.

I worried Josh was planning to keep our involvement here brief, cutting things off before we could do anything substantial about the problem. He had seemed unconvinced by the evidence, which worried me more, but maybe it would sink in after a while. Denial is a natural first response to encountering things in which we don't believe, or don't wish to believe. Josh needed to move beyond that.

Eventually, I pulled the drapes tight and stretched out on the other bottom bunk. I slept fitfully through the morning, my exhaustion competing against my feelings of apprehension about this place, which never quite faded away.

It was a relief to wake up, or at least give up on fitful in-and-out drowsing, and get back to work.

The gentle whine of a circular saw greeted me as my cellphone alarm beeped me awake.

Stacey appeared undisturbed by the saw and the alarm, sleeping in an improbable position, one arm draped over the front of her bunk, one foot out of bed and on the floor.

"Get up, Snorey Smurf." I jostled her shoulder. "We have to wire our clients' bedroom for sound and video. Which is weird to say."

"But I don't snore," Stacey protested.

Looking out the window, I found the source of the sawing. At the far end of the cabin circle, Josh and his sons stood near Warthog Cabin, one of those that remained in poor condition from years of neglect.

After popping open a can of cold coffee from our travel cooler, I hurried to throw on jeans, a tank top, and my leather jacket—most entities won't attack during the day, but I wanted a little armor just in case. I snapped on my utility belt for the same reason.

"Get ready to meet the kids," I told Stacey a minute later, as we brushed our teeth. "We have to stick with the promotional videographer angle, it sounds like. I kind of hate lying, though. It takes so much effort to keep the lies straight."

"Well, I do have a film degree, you know," she said. "Hey, we actually *could* make them a promotional video while we're at it. I'll make it sound even better than Camp Mizpah. Though it's clearly, you know, not. But that way—"

"We don't have to lie to the kids," I said. "As much."

"Right."

"I like it. Especially if you do the work part of that, and all I have to do is the agreeing part."

We stepped outside. The whole family was out there. While Josh and his two teenage sons worked with the power tools to restore Bobcat Cabin, Allison sat on the stoop of Falcon Cabin and read a book to seven-year-old Shiloh, who knelt in the dirt arranging pine needles and cones into patterns. It was unclear whether the girl was listening at all.

"There they are!" Josh grinned through a layer of sawdust as he approached us. I recognized the kids from the picture in Allison's office, though they were older now.

The boy at his side, with the blond buzzcut and the Atlanta Braves tank top, had to be fourteen-year-old Nate, his grin even wider than his father's, as if he, too, had a timeshare to sell us.

The older boy, Ephraim, hung back at the work site. He was paler, his hair long and ratty, his black Rise Against t-shirt loose on his frame. He looked like he would have been more at home moping around the back corner of a dark club, maybe wearing a spiky dog collar. Anywhere but out in the fresh air and sunshine doing carpentry.

"These are the filmmakers," Josh told Nate as they approached us, overly loud as if not-so-subtly reminding Stacey and me of our cover story. I was already feeling more comfortable with Stacey's plan to keep ourselves honest by actually making the video. "Miss Ellie and Miss Stacey."

"You don't have to call me Miss—" Stacey began.

"Good to meet you." Nate, nearly as tall as his father and with a similar cocky grin, seized my hand and shook it. He turned and shook Stacey's a bit longer, beaming at her the way guys do, and being no more subtle about it than his father had been about our cover story. "And definitely good to meet you."

"Uh, hi," Stacey said, gradually taking her hand back.

"Ephraim, manners! Come say hello!" Josh barked at the distant sixteen-year-old, who reluctantly slogged his way over. He stopped several paces away.

"Nice to meet you there, Ephraim," Stacey said.

Ephraim gave a half-hearted wave, glancing between us. "So are we done for the day?" he asked his dad.

"Done for the day?" Josh was plainly exasperated. He gave me an over-the-top headshake like he couldn't believe what he was hearing from his son, and for some reason wanted to drag me into it. "Did you not listen to the game plan? Was quitting early in the game plan? Were you staring at your phone again?"

"Uh, no, we aren't allowed to *have* phones at the work site," Ephraim said. "So how could I—"

"We'll table this for later," Josh interrupted. "Like I said, guys, your only job is to stay completely out of these ladies' way. Don't bother them at all."

Ephraim shrugged and focused on toeing at a patch of weeds with his shoe.

"But we can help them if they need it, right?" Nate said, tearing his eyes from Stacey to look at his dad. "Like to carry stuff, or if they want a guide. I've explored more than anyone else. I can help you find your way no matter how dark it is." He looked back at Stacey and raised his sawdust-coated eyebrows.

"That's very generous of you, Nathan, and I appreciate your positive attitude." Josh looked mostly at Ephraim while he said this. Ephraim was still peering into the weeds and kicking the dirt. "Let's get back to work. Ephraim, go watch your sister. Take over for your mom."

Ephraim shrugged and ambled toward Falcon Cabin, where Allison stood and waved us over. Shiloh continued playing with the twigs, stones, and pine straw on the ground in front of the cabin, not seeming to notice or care that her mother had stopped reading.

"We'll head over there, too," I told Josh. "Nice to meet you, Nathan."

"Thanks. Excellent jacket." He pointed at me and waved before he left.

"He talks a lot," Ephraim said, almost under his breath,

as we walked together. "Sorry."

"Which one do you mean? Your dad or your brother?" I asked, and Ephraim laughed instead of answering. He gave me an appreciative look, like someone finally understood what he was dealing with daily.

Shiloh did not look up from her sticks and stones project as we approached. Shiloh's hair was sandy and unruly, despite the braid her mother had attempted to create from it. Her large, dark eyes stared intently at her project, her lips pressed together, deadly serious.

"Ephraim, can you finish Shy's history lesson?" Allison held the book out to him while he took her place on the cabin's small covered stoop. "Just to the end of the chapter. Then the questions. She can write in crayon if she wants."

"Okay." Ephraim deadpanned the word as he took the illustrated history from his mom. He looked at the page. "Hey, Shy, want to hear about princesses?"

"No," Shy answered.

"Not even medieval ax-wielding princesses who hack up evil knights?"

"Josh, don't scare her!" Allison snapped, but Shiloh giggled.

"Medieval ax-wielding prin-cess-es!" Shiloh sang out, abandoning her project to clamber onto the porch and gaze at the history book. "Medieval ax-wielding—"

"Let's go," Allison said to Stacey and me, shaking her head.

We hiked up the trail to the main lodge. Allison had parked her SUV by our van.

We followed her out of the corner of the parking lot, past a faded Do Not Enter sign and onto a bumpy, largely washed-out gravel road winding around the outside of camp, well away from the trails.

Trees were thick on either side, but we also got a look at some of the camp's less rustic features, like a small power station and pumphouse. We skirted around a steep, wooded face of Stony Owl Hill.

The gravel road curved sharply before ending at the caretaker's cottage, where the back yard backed up to the hill.

"We need to get this done as fast as possible," Allison said as she opened the back door to let us inside. "The kids shouldn't be back for a couple of hours, but things can go wrong."

In her bedroom, I took a moment to study the layout.

"We can do this discreetly, so it's not obvious even if your kids look in here," I said. "One camera in your closet, angled to face the windows. Maybe one under the bed. A microphone, too, if you don't mind."

"Sounds good," Allison said, looking at the window where she'd seen the shadow figure enter her home. "It was so tall. Like a walking tree."

"Hopefully we'll catch some video of it."

"Not that Josh would believe it. You saw how he reacted to what you found last night. Personally, I got the chills when I saw those things moving in the attic. What do y'all think it is?" she asked, lowering her voice. "Is it really a... you know? Could this place really be haunted?"

"Lots of places are haunted," I said. "The question is whether it amounts to more than a nuisance—maybe a frightening nuisance—or something truly dangerous."

"So is it dangerous?"

I hesitated. "It's definitely a strong presence. It's much larger, physically, than what we typically see. That doesn't mean it's malevolent. But if it's powerful enough to move objects, we need to learn more about it."

As we set up, Stacey talked about her idea for a promotional video. "It'll be fun, and we can sidestep the whole dishonesty aspect."

"That would be great. I don't like lying to the kids, either. I feel like Ephraim may have seen something. Maybe he'll talk to one of you about it. You're much closer to his age. He's been distant with us for a while."

"I bet I can warm him up," Stacey said. "You just have to ask questions they can relate to. Like, do you play Minecraft? Or, have you played Minecraft lately? Or, say, how's about that Minecraft?"

"He... *does* like Minecraft, actually. Or he used to. It's hard to keep up with what he's interested in." She stepped out of the room. "I'll be over on the back porch if you need me."

Stacey and I hurried to set up as quickly and discreetly as we could. We tested the gear from the van.

"Problem," Stacey said, looking up at the monitors in the van. "I can access the wireless feeds from Allison's room while we're parked here, but the signal from the lodge is poor to nonexistent. We're not set up to work over such wide distances. The big hill isn't doing us any favors."

"That's too bad," I said. "We'll just have to drive to different observation points during the night."

"Like storm chasers searching for a tornado."

"Sure." We walked to the screened porch in back, where Allison worked on her laptop at a wobbly old picnic table.

"All set here," I told her through the screen. "Everything will record tonight. We're heading to the cabins. Maybe we'll pick up some sign of activity in Bobcat Cabin. Or the people your daughter was talking about. I'd like to hear her version of things."

"She'll only tell you if she's in a talking mood. No guarantees. And whatever she says, take it with some salt."

Stacey and I drove to the main lodge parking lot, then lugged gear down the long walk to the boys' cabin area. Thankfully there was a slight downhill grade all the way to the lake. Hauling the gear back up after the investigation would be a hassle, though.

I slowed as we reached the cabins. "Where is everyone?"

The tools were still out, but Josh and the three kids had vanished like Roanoke Colony settlers.

"This is weird," Stacey said. She looked toward the woods on the far side, toward the path down to the lake. "Do you hear that?"

Distantly, a man's voice called out.

"What's he saying?" I asked.

"Shy!" This voice was closer, accompanied by footsteps in crunching leaves.

As Stacey and I reached the central clearing with the fire ring, Ephraim stumbled down from the steep tree-lined slope at one side of the cabin circle. He yelled again: "Shiloh!" He cast a nervous glance at us and began to swerve wide, like he was planning to avoid us altogether.

"What's happening?" I asked him.

"Uh." He nearly tripped over his own feet as he changed course toward us. "My sister. Have you seen her? She disappeared."

"No, sorry. We'll help look as soon as we put our stuff down," I said, hurrying toward Wolf Cabin as fast as I could with all the stuff I was carrying, which was not very fast at all.

We dropped off our gear just inside the cabin door. I heard Josh's voice calling for Shiloh somewhere in the distance. Ephraim was still close by, looking into the windows of the cabins.

"Where did you last see her?" I asked.

"Over there." He pointed to the porch with the girl's school work heaped on the stoop. "She was just sitting there monkeying around with the pine cones, and I was reading her history book. Then I looked up and she was gone. Dad and Nate went to look for her near the lake. Because, you know. She's not a great swimmer."

"You already checked all the cabins?" I asked.

"We called into each one. She didn't answer." Ephraim looked panicked. "I didn't hear her walk away. She didn't *say* anything. I couldn't watch her and read the book at the same time. That's two things, and I only have two eyes, and they don't swivel independently, so—"

"Let's split up and search each cabin," I said. "Look in every closet and under every bunk bed."

I headed for Bobcat Cabin. The door stood open; it would have been easy for the girl to quietly sneak inside.

I stepped through the doorway.

"Shiloh?" I called. The window's heavy canvas curtains were drawn and the light switch didn't respond, so I clicked on my flashlight.

The layout was the same as Wolf Cabin. I'd entered a common room. Where our cabin had new, recently painted drywall, everything here looked like it hadn't been touched in decades.

"Hey, I know we haven't met," I said. "I'm Ellie. I'm

here to help. Are you okay? Shiloh?"

I heard something toward the back of the cabin, where the bedrooms were. A single thump. Maybe an animal, but a small one. Or a small girl.

"Shiloh?"

I crossed the common room and entered the hallway. As in our cabin, the hall ran across the middle of the cabin, dividing the front half from the back. The bathroom door was directly ahead, flanked on either side by the bedroom doors.

"Are you there?" I asked, sweeping the hallway and its doors with my flashlight. "Hello?"

From off to the right came a brief scraping sound, like something heavy dragging across the hardwood floor, but only for a moment.

It was enough, though. I started off for the right-hand bedroom.

I eased the door open and shined my light in. I didn't see anybody. There were a pair of skeletal bunk bed frames with no mattresses. One seemed slightly askew. Streaks in the heavy dust on the floor indicated it had moved recently.

A rusty squeak sounded ahead, and I walked toward it.

Beyond the bunk bed was a closet with narrow folding doors and rusty hinges.

"I know you're in there," I said. "Game's over. You can come out now."

She giggled behind the door. It was brief, like she'd clapped a hand over her mouth, but it had rung out clear as a bell in the quiet room.

"Okay, Shiloh. Here I come."

I stepped forward and opened the closet.

I didn't hesitate, because some part of me expected to

see something awful when I opened it. Perhaps instead of Shiloh, the girl with the messy hair and dark eyes, I would see some horrible apparition. It would obviously not be the first time in my life something like that has happened. The best I could hope was for something shadowy instead of gory, that I wouldn't see a dead person swinging from a noose or missing half his head from a century-old gunshot wound.

Nothing like that waited inside the closet, though. There was nothing at all in there but loose boards, rusty nails, and fallen shelves.

"Hello?" I asked, though I seemed to be alone in here after all. I knelt, shining my flashlight into the closet.

Behind the collapsed shelves, the back of the closet had several missing boards. Shiloh could have crawled through there, into the dark space beyond.

I crawled into the closet and shifted aside boards for a better view.

Beyond the gap in the wall lay another room strewn with more loose boards. Some had rusty nails jutting out of them; it wasn't exactly a safe area for a kid to crawl around. Or for me, either.

"Hello?" I said again. My light found more bunk beds; I was looking into the other bedroom through the broken-down closet door. I didn't see anybody in there.

I heard something, though—footsteps clattering out of sight, along with more giggles. Running away from me. It was a girl, hard to tell her age.

Since there was zero chance of me trying to climb over rusty nails through the hole in the back of the closet, I hopped up and ran to intercept the girl in the hallway.

But nobody was there. The door to the other bedroom

was slightly ajar.

"Shiloh?" I approached the door and eased it open.

There was nobody in the second bedroom. I'd half-expected it by that point, having encountered nothing but empty rooms so far, but it was still disquieting.

I checked the bathroom and counselor's room. Despite what I'd heard, I was the only person in the building .

"Okay," I said, trying to project confidence toward whatever entity was toying with me, though I was very uncomfortable being alone in there with an unseen laughing thing. "You win. Game's over."

I clicked off my flashlight and walked backward across the common room, keeping my back to the open front door and my eyes on the dark hallway. I didn't want any giggling little demons sneaking up behind me as I tried to leave.

"Want to come out and say hello?" I asked the darkness.

Did something move back there in the hallway? Maybe.

"Ellie!" Stacey's voice called outside. "Ellie, we found her."

"See you later," I told the invisible presence before I stepped out of the cabin.

Stacey and Ephraim were walking toward me with Shiloh between them, green weeds in her hair, dirt all over her face and sundress. She smiled impishly.

"I found her under the stairs at Warthog Cabin," Stacey said. "She said she was playing hide and seek."

"Who were you playing with?" I asked, still shivering from my unexpected ghostly encounter. The cabin door stood open behind me; I hurried down off the stoop to get away from it.

Shiloh shrugged and opened her mouth.

"Nobody. She didn't tell us she was hiding," Ephraim said. "You're going to be in so much trouble, Shy."

The girl frowned, her expression reminding me of her mother talking about her troubles. Whatever she'd been about to say, she swallowed it back and stayed quiet.

"Did you tell your father she's been found?" I asked Ephraim, and he gave me the reaction I wanted.

"Oh! I better go." He loped off down the trail, thin and gangly and not particularly fast.

"Shiloh," I said, when he was away, "who were you playing with?"

"Just the kids." She took me in with her deep, dark eyes. "They want to know who you are."

"My name is Ellie," I said. "And this is Stacey. We're just taking pictures and video around here for your mom and dad."

"Hi!" Stacey said, waving and kind of overdoing it, as bubbly as fresh-popped champagne.

Shiloh looked at her, then back to me. "Okay."

"What kids, Shy?" I asked.

She wandered off in the direction her brother had gone, but without any sense of hurry. She veered toward the fire ring instead and walked on the circle of stone, darkened on the inside by countless years of use, though it had sat cold and empty in recent years. In past generations, it had been a gathering spot for stories and teaching, a kind of ritual space for half-grown kids who found themselves midway between the mythic imagination of childhood and the responsible buttoned-down adult world, still young enough to be innocent and wild for the summer.

"Shiloh," I said. "What kids?"

The girl gestured vaguely around, saying nothing.

"Can you see the kids? Or hear them?"

No answer. I decided to go a different route: "Do you always see people that the rest of your family can't see?"

Shiloh didn't reply. She hummed to herself as she walked around the top of the stone ring, hands out to her sides for balance.

"Shy!" her father called as he emerged from the woods, Nate at his side, Ephraim trailing several paces behind them.

The girl didn't even look over. She was lost in her own humming, staring at the blackened ground of the fire pit as though entranced.

"Shiloh, where did you go?" Josh bellowed. His face was red, and he was fuming. He was definitely not in timeshare-selling mode. "We've been looking all over!"

Shiloh scrunched up at his voice, drawing her shoulders in and wincing as if she'd been struck.

"She was playing hide and seek," Ephraim told his dad.

"You were supposed to be watching her!" Josh said.

"How could I watch her and read at the same time? Human eyes don't swivel independently, Dad."

"What are you talking about, weirdo?" Nathan snorted.

"Don't start driving down Attitude Avenue, Ephraim," Josh said. "You're grounded."

"From what? Labor camp?" Ephraim looked at the work site around the cabin.

"Yeah, very funny, Ephraim. You're a real clown." Josh looked our way, seemed to recall we were there, and moderated his tone. "We'll talk about this later. Take your sister home. Try not to lose her on the way."

I was disappointed to watch Ephraim and Shiloh

trudge off quietly. According to their mom, they were the two who'd most likely encountered the strange and supernatural here at the camp. I wanted to talk to them at length.

Instead, I was left with Josh, who put on his big smile and his sales voice, and Nate, who stood alongside him, arms folded in the same way, wearing a smile that was closer to a smirk. The fourteen-year-old was mainly looking at Stacey.

"Sorry about that," Josh told me. "Shy gets off in her own world. Sometimes we have to pull her back. Anyway, how's the, uh, project looking? Think we'll get some promising video?"

"Looks very interesting so far."

"How long do you imagine it will take to complete?" Josh asked. "Remember, I'm willing to pay extra for speed."

"We're going as fast as we can," I said. "Hopefully just a few days. It's hard to know at this point."

Josh nodded, not looking satisfied by my answer. "The sooner the better. We'd better get back to the house."

"I can come back and build a fire," Nate said. He bit his lip, a rare sign of vulnerability from him, and shifted his gaze from Stacey to the fire pit. "If you're staying, you should have one."

"That would be great!" Stacey said, probably just genuinely pleased by the idea of a campfire. I wish she hadn't, because I'd already opened my mouth to politely decline. After Stacey spoke, though, I didn't want to come off rude by contradicting her.

"Very generous of you, Nathan," Josh said.

I sighed, but only inwardly. "As long as it's not too late."

Josh and Nathan packed up their worksite, padlocking their heavier tools and generator inside a cabin before leaving.

"Let's set up before Junior Scout comes back to build you a fire," I told Stacey.

"I think it'll be nice to have a campfire. It will really tune us into the place. At Camp Mizpah the fire was like the heart of it all. We'd gather round, drink cider, sing songs—"

"No songs. Come on. We need to keep an eye on Bobcat Cabin, too. I heard things in there." I filled her in as we set up observation gear.

"Do you think it was the same entity from the lodge?" Stacey asked.

"I don't know; we'll compare data when we have it. But that's two encounters in less than twenty-four hours. This place is starting to look like a hotbed of paranormal activity. Now we just have to figure out why, and whether any of it threatens our clients and their kids."

Standing inside our cabin, I adjusted the angle of the night vision camera trained on Bobcat Cabin, the one that had been mysteriously damaged in the night, the one with the invisible laughing entity who'd played its own game of hide and seek with me. Maybe I'd been part of the game with Shiloh and the ghosts of dead children, without even knowing it until it was over.

Chapter Eleven

By the time the sun was low and out of sight, we were ready. We had a camera and microphone inside Bobcat Cabin, hoping to catch some readings of the invisible giggler. We watched the outdoors by way of cameras looking out our cabin windows.

In the second bedroom of our cabin, Stacey set up tablets and a laptop as a mini-nerve center, because we couldn't bring the van any closer than the parking lot up at the lodge.

From here, we could watch the feeds from surrounding cabins, but the feeds from the lodge and the caretaker's cabin where the family lived were sporadic. The thick woods and huge hill weren't helpful. There was no WiFi around the cabins for us to piggyback on because the campers' cabins were meant to be completely screen-free; screen time was only available at the lodge and at the

Conner family home.

As we finalized the second-bedroom nerve center, someone knocked on our front door.

Nate stood out there. He cast Stacey a smile and an eyebrow raise. It was pretty ridiculous. Probably worked on girls his age, though.

"I brought some serious wood," he told her. "It's going to be a sweet fire. Probably blaze all night."

Out at the fire ring, Ephraim was silently transferring a heap of limbs and small logs from a wheelbarrow, with the grim look of a gravedigger or a Dickensian factory worker condemned to long hours in horrible conditions.

"Looks great!" Stacey said, being way too positive about it.

"We don't want it to blaze all night," I told Nate. "Maybe twenty, twenty-five minutes of blazing, tops." I closed the door and sighed at Stacey. "Hopefully they have something worthwhile to tell us."

"No need to be so glum. Just take a few minutes to kick back and enjoy the fire and the scenery."

"You're right. I will be done with that after just a few minutes. Don't forget to refresh your bug spray." I looked through the windows at the boys bickering with each other as they arranged the firewood. "This seems potentially awkward."

"I thought we'd want to hear from all the family members."

"And we do. So let's get it over with."

"That's not a happy camper attitude!" Stacey said. "Let's approach this challenge with Mizpah confidence and Mizpah cheer!"

"I'll handle the confidence, you handle the cheer. Just

get them talking about ghosts if you can."

"No problemo."

We went out to join them. I sat on a boulder while Nate worked to light the tepee of kindling he'd built. Ephraim waved his phone around, trying unsuccessfully to find a signal. He was clearly only there because there was nothing else to do.

"Nice work," Stacey told Nate as the younger but more muscular boy started the fire. "Have you done a lot of camping?"

"Yeah, Boy Scouts," Nate said. "I'm working towards Eagle Scout. College admissions lap that stuff up like thirsty poodles. But Effie quit scouting back in Webelos. No college application fatteners for him."

"Don't call me Effie," Ephraim muttered, almost robotically, like he'd said it a thousand times before.

"Effie Effingham." Nate smirked, and Ephraim replied with a rude hand gesture. Nate looked at Stacey. "Don't mind my brother. He's a class-W weirdo. He's probably scared to talk to you because you're a girl."

"Shut up, Nathan."

"Ooh, I'm shaking in my shorts," Nate said. "What are you going to do, Effie, whine at me?"

"Maybe we should leave," I said, rising from my boulder. It was after nightfall. Darkness gathered around us on all sides, beyond the circle of the fire's red glow, like black curtains closing over the campground.

"No! Hey, it's fine." Nate jumped up from his crouch near the fire and stepped over to me. I almost thought he would grab my arm, but he didn't. He spoke in a smooth, calming tone like I was a nervous horse on the verge of panicking, or a potential sucker trying to leave his pyramid scheme presentation early. "Everything's cool here. We'll be chill and have fun. Y'all stay."

"Why don't you guys tell us more about the camp?" Stacey asked.

"You mean you haven't heard enough from my dad?" Nate hurried to give Stacey his full attention. He returned to his seat, a sideways slab of tree trunk the size of a park bench. "I figured he'd be loading you down with stories about the old days."

"Not really. The old days?" I asked. "What do you mean by that? The camp's history?"

"Right. When he used to come here every summer. He took the archery first-place ribbon—"

"—two years in a row," Ephraim interrupted, his voice barely a mumble.

"Is that why your father wanted this place, you think?" I asked, stunned by this new information. "Because he came here as a kid?"

"Oh, yeah," Nathan said. "Mom wanted this big farm near Lake Hartwell but Dad was like, no, *this* is the spot. Dad even sings the song when we're out working on stuff. 'Old Stony Owl... stand watchful, nosy, and true—'"

"*Noble*," Ephraim said. "Nosy doesn't even make sense."

"Who cares? Stacey, Ellie, ladies, have some marshmallows." Nathan reached for the cooler, and of course Stacey agreed, and soon they were both roasting the puffy sugary lumps over the flames. Nate held his up like a torch when it caught fire, shriveling and blackening inside its nimbus of raw flame. "Check that out!" he shouted; he couldn't have been more enthusiastic if he were watching a giant fireworks display. His energy was almost infectious.

I looked over at Ephraim, who was quietly rolling a small rock between his fingers, staring at it intently, in the manner of a kid bored out of his mind. The red light of the fire overtook the paleness of his face and the redness of his acne, giving him a different look. Healthier.

"So what can you tell us about this place, Ephraim?" I asked.

"I don't know." He looked up at me briefly, but his gaze quickly skittered off me and out toward the ever-darkening woods. Night had definitely fallen now. "It's old."

"Oh, is it *old*?" Nate mocked his older brother's voice. "Wow, they could never have figured out it was *old*. There's only a *museum* about how *old* it is."

Ephraim just glared at him, seemingly unable to respond.

"This place is kinda spooky to me," Stacey said. "When I was a kid, my summer camp had a legend about a camper that died on the archery course. They said you could sometimes see her out at night, with the arrow still stuck in her chest, still bleeding. Arrowhead Annie. If you didn't get away fast, she'd shoot you, too." She paused and looked out into the woods. "Have you ever wondered if this place was haunted?"

"Well, our dad did tell us the one legend," Ephraim said. "The story is that the Stony Owl is really a graveyard for old Native American warriors, and one of them was assigned to guard Stony Owl for all time. So he walks the trails at night, and anyone who goes up there and gets too close to the owl... well, he hunts them down, because he's a master hunter, and then he hacks them to pieces. They call him the Trailwalker. And if you go sneaking up to the owl late at night, he'll get you. Once he starts tracking you, he never stops. Not until you're dead. He'll even follow you home, no matter how far it is."

"Yeah, right." Nate shook his head and slurped down his second charred marshmallow. "There's nothing scary about this place. Effy got scared when we moved here, though." He snickered and jabbed two marshmallows onto the tip of his extendable steel roasting stick. His mouth was ringed with white goop and black crust.

"Really?" I looked at Ephraim with interest while trying to sound casual. "Have you seen anything strange since moving here?"

"Oh, yeah," Nate snickered. "Every time he looks in the mirror."

"Shut up, Nathan," Ephraim grumbled, without much force at all.

"That's all you ever say," Nathan replied. "'Shut up. Shut up.' Like you want everyone to act like you, sitting around being quiet and creepy and staring at people."

"I'm not staring at anyone."

"You're being creepy though."

"This is stupid. I'm going home." Ephraim stood up and trudged away.

"Good," Nathan said. "You're embarrassing me anyway. You always have to complain and kill any fun. You suck the fun out of everything, every time. Party killer!"

"What party?" Ephraim tossed over his shoulder.

"I'll walk with you." I jogged over to join Ephraim. He wasn't moving very fast.

"Good idea, he might get scared by himself," Nathan said.

"No, I won't." Ephraim picked up the pace.

"I wanted to hear what you were going to say," I told him as we followed the wooded trail from the campground to the lake, in a low voice so his brother couldn't hear.

"Wasn't going to say anything." He kept his eyes on the trail ahead, lit by his flashlight.

"About something scaring you here at the campground."

"No. I wasn't scared. My brother's just stupid."

"But something did happen?" I felt like I was grasping at straws on a cart that was pulling away. "Something unusual? I want to hear."

"No. I mean maybe I thought I saw somebody, but they weren't there. It couldn't have been real anyway."

"That sounds interesting. What did you see?"

"Doesn't matter."

"I'd really like to hear it."

"Why?"

"I like ghost stories."

He slowed down and looked over at me, like he was trying to tell if I was kidding or not.

"Okay," he said. "It wasn't far from here, actually. I was out here walking after dinner one night, because I really needed space from everyone."

"Totally understandable."

We walked around the lake, keeping back to avoid the muddy shore.

"Up here." He pointed to the trail marked STONY OWL EFFIGY. "That's where I saw it."

"What did you see?" I pointed my flashlight up the steep trail, thinking of our walk up there with Allison.

"First, I heard a strange howl," he said. "Then something running toward me from the woods. And then, whoa! A pack of werewolves with glowing red eyes. Riding, um, motorcycles."

"Uh-huh."

"I'm just *kidding*. I haven't really seen anything. But it's definitely weird out here, isn't it? Like you can almost..."

"Almost what?"

"I don't know. It's just, well, if you go outside alone late at night, when everyone else is asleep, just look around and listen. It's like there really is something out there watching you. I don't mean the owls and junk, you know there's going to be animals out there. But it's kind of like... did you ever read *Lord of the Flies* in school?"

"I did."

"It's like the beast, the one nobody sees but everybody feels. The one the hunters make sacrifices to. When I look out in the woods at night, that's what it feels like. The beast."

His description chilled me. I thought of the large, unexplained cold spot that moved objects in the lodge attic. I also thought of boys trapped in the wild on a remote island, their attempts at peace and civilization crumbling as they watched the wilderness for a nameless evil.

"That can't be a pleasant feeling," I said.

"Well, in the book, the beast wasn't real," he said. "Or it was real but it was inside the boys. They brought the evil with them. Right?"

"Yeah. I think that's right."

"So I tell myself it's in my head, like in that book, but that doesn't feel completely right. But it doesn't feel completely wrong, either." He slowed as the path reached the sprawling caretaker's cottage, the building that had grown too large over the years to really call a cottage, but in such slapdash and mismatched fashion that it was hard to call it anything fancier.

"Personally," I said, "I believe in ghosts. So if you ever want to talk about anything, I'll listen."

"Ever?" He stopped short of the long rectangles of light cast from the glowing windows of the cottage. The clearing around it had no real lawn, just gravel and raised garden beds full of weeds, their wooden retaining walls crumbling. "How long are you staying? I thought you were just making a commercial."

"Well, we want enough footage to have plenty of options. My partner Stacey also really likes camping. She'd probably be somewhere in the woods if she wasn't working. Doing wildlife photography. So this is like a vacation for her."

"But not for you?"

"Not as much," I said, and he laughed.

"Yeah, my dad keeps saying this place is like living in a resort. It's more like what's left of a resort after a natural disaster or something. Maybe a flood. Or an earthquake." He sighed as he looked at the sprawling cottage's deep-set front door shadowed by its low, hooded front porch roof, built in the same style as the main lodge. "I better go."

"Okay. It was good talking to you."

He looked startled by this. "Really?"

"Of course. Why wouldn't it be?"

"I don't know. Sorry. We're kind of stuck out here alone. I haven't seen anybody else in forever. So that's probably why I seem so weird."

"You don't—"

"Bye." He hurried inside, as if I'd done something to panic him. I'm not super great with people. Maybe Stacey was having better luck with the other guy.

The walk back around seemed longer when I was alone, the trail skirting the edges of Stony Owl Hill and the lake. I turned off my flashlight so I could get a better sense of the place, doing my best to navigate by the pale beams of moonlight that leaked down through the towering trees.

Insects sang in the woods, but it otherwise was quiet, perhaps too early in the night for the owls. Alone for the moment, I could really feel how isolated we were out here in the mountains, miles from the nearest town. How close were the campground's nearest neighbors? If someone screamed, would anybody hear? Probably not.

It was hard not to think of what Ephraim had said, and perhaps he'd hurried away afterward because he felt he'd exposed too much of his feelings. The beast, lurking in the dark, just out of sight.

Lord of the Flies had, of course, been named for the demon Beelzebub, sometimes identified as the devil himself, sometimes as a different but powerful demon. As a gloomy and depressed teenager unhealthily obsessed with death and the macabre, I'd read more about such things than the average person really ought to.

The invisible beast of the wild, or at least the idea of it, stalked me all the way back to the cabins.

Chapter Twelve

"So that was how we came back in the ninth," Nate was saying as I returned to the camp. I heard him before I could see him; he and Stacey were on the other side of the fire. "I hit it over the fence for a triple. This pitcher's balls would dip at the last second, very tricky, you had to adjust for that..."

The fire was larger than I remembered, as if Nate had been feeding it more wood, really dragging things out. As long as we had to hide our true job from the clients' kids, we couldn't really get to work until Nate was gone.

"Anybody else getting sleepy?" I asked, faking a yawn as I arrived.

"Didn't y'all sleep all morning?" Nate asked.

"Not really," I said, which was kind of true because I hadn't slept all that well.

"How was your walk?" Stacey asked.

"It got pretty eerie on the way back." I checked for a reaction from Nate. "Do you ever find this place scary at night? Or haunted, like in the legend?"

"I'm not scared." Nate crossed his arms. "This place is great. There's not many people to hang out with, but it's going to blow up when it opens for summer. Girls everywhere. Plus I'll get paid the whole time."

I nodded along, reflecting on my utter failure to extract anything like a ghost story out of this kid.

"Nate's been mapping the mountain," Stacey said.

"Yeah, for my Geology badge. I've been all over. I know these woods better than my dad, even."

"Have you found anything interesting out there?" I asked. "Anything unusual?"

He smirked, and I felt a little irritated by the expression. "Oh, yeah."

"Like what?" Stacey asked.

Nate looked at her and shrugged, his smirk fading a little. "No big deal really. Like for one thing, there's an island where the creek meets the lake; you can only get to it over this one fallen tree, which isn't that easy. Effie probably couldn't handle it, not that he's ever tried. It's better during the day, though. You don't want to go to the lake at night."

"Why not?" I asked.

"Uh, it's just hard to see and slippery. There's rocks in the creek. You don't want to fall." Nate was starting to sound evasive, which naturally made me want to know more. "Anyway, daytime, I'll take you there if you want." He stood up and brushed off his khaki shorts. "I should get going."

His sudden departure surprised me; I'd had the

impression he was digging in for a long night of hanging out and eyeballing Stacey. I was glad to be wrong.

"Bye," I told him. "Be safe."

"Yeah, I've walked this path a million times. Later on, Stacey." He gave her a finger gun before walking off toward the trail. The glow of his flashlight floated away into the woods like a will o' the wisp.

"I think that kid's got a crush on you," I said to Stacey.

"He didn't have one remotely supernatural experience, as far as I could fish out of him. He only talked about sports and parties and where he wants to go to college and girls he's dated. Any luck with the other guy?"

"Ephraim finds the campground unpleasant, but he didn't seem to have specific encounters with anything. Or maybe he did, but backed off telling me directly. He talked about *Lord of the Flies* and the beast they thought was haunting the island."

"But it turned out to be a pig, right? Like a talking pig? Or was that *Charlotte's Web*?"

"They both had talking pigs. Very different ones. Should we put this fire out and head inside?"

"I was going to brew some coffee first. Couldn't do it in front of the kid since we're hiding our nocturnal activities."

"Good thinking. On both counts."

Stacey set up a steel camping percolator that steamed in the campfire, and soon poured hot, dark coffee into my travel mug. It tasted strong enough to fuel a truck driver for a nonstop cross-country haul. "Well, that opened my eyes," I told her.

We lingered by the campfire longer than I'd intended. With the boys gone, it was actually kind of peaceful and pleasant; the crackling of the burning logs, the stars growing visible above the clearing where we sat.

But beyond our little pool of firelight lay a vast darkness full of things unseen.

"So Allison's the only person who's actually encountered anything strange," I said, thinking aloud when the silence started to eat at me. "And maybe the little girl, but she's not exactly a chatterbox."

"And you," Stacey said

"And me." I looked over at Bobcat Cabin, where I'd chased the invisible thing that sounded like a laughing child. "I wonder if our microphone's picked up the giggler."

"I wonder if those boys are really telling us everything." Stacey refilled my coffee cup, then her own. "That's the last of the coffee. Ready to quash the fire?"

After shoveling dirt over it, we headed inside to watch and listen.

On a screen that gave us an exterior thermal-camera view of the boys' cabin area, the campfire area still glowed dull red under the soil we'd smothered it with.

Other monitors showed the shadowy bedrooms in Bobcat Cabin. Our microphone in the broken-down closet connecting the bedrooms picked up only occasional creaks and groans and a distant chorus of night insects. Maybe it would catch a few giggles later.

"Not much happening at the moment," Stacey said. "I wonder if the lodge cameras are picking up anything like last night. That attic seemed like a gold mine of paranormal activity." She frowned. "Well, 'gold mine' doesn't sound right. Maybe a silver mine. That's more ghostly, don't you think?"

"Don't you think it's strange Josh has never mentioned

coming here during his childhood?" I asked, dropping onto my bunk.

"Maybe he's mentioned it enough that Allison's tired of hearing it, so he didn't say it aloud. He doesn't really take our investigation seriously anyway. Even after we showed him evidence."

"We need to get his guard down and learn about his personal history with this place. Away from his family, so there's no interruptions."

I focused on watching the inside and outside of the dilapidated Bobcat Cabin, listening carefully for giggles, footsteps, or anything else that shouldn't have been present in the shadowy old building.

Chapter Thirteen

For a long while, all we caught on the camera was intermittent swells of blue as cold mountain winds blew through the campground, rustling leaves and pushing the aged timbers of the cabins until they creaked.

The open door to Bobcat Cabin squeaked and banged in the wind. I was tempted to go out and close it tight—each bang boomed through our speakers—but I was not eager for another visit with the invisible giggler.

After a couple of hours, I grew restless from the lack of activity. "Let's take a walk up to the lodge."

"Yeah, finally!" Stacey jumped to her feet and pulled on a denim jacket. "The lodge is where it's at." She'd been chomping to go up there for a while, hoping our equipment had recorded more activity in the attic.

We stepped out of Wolf Cabin into a cool night with a chilly breeze. Stacey stuck close by my side as we walked over to Bobcat Cabin and secured the front door so it would stop banging in the wind.

The trail up to the lodge was dark under the tree canopy. Unseen creatures rustled overhead, as if plotting to pounce on us from above. Owls hooted; the sprawl of branches seemed full of the birds. It sounded like a whole owl city up there.

We emerged into the moonlit clearing around the huge central fire pit where all trails converged. The main lodge waited ahead, seeming larger at night, its aged wooden walls even darker, the moonlight scarcely casting a glow across its roof.

"The place sure looks like it would have a ghost in the attic." Stacey looked up with apprehension at one of the few small windows on the second floor. She seemed less enthusiastic about the lodge the closer we got.

We skirted the edges of the lodge, keeping out of its shadow, emerging into the parking lot where our van waited near the lodge's front entrance. The van was a welcome sight, a little dash of home in this unnerving environment.

"Ah," Stacey said, as if feeling the same when she climbed into the van. She brought a few of the built-in monitors to life, showing us locations in and around the main lodge. The windows again stood open in the office, stiff canvas curtains swaying in the breeze. "I wonder if we caught anything up here."

"Feel free to start looking." I opened my laptop and connected to the lodge's weak WiFi signal, providing satellite internet.

Unfortunately, the signal was intentionally weak, meant primarily for the office area, in keeping with the Conners' general anti-screen policy for the camp. I was trying to access online newspaper archives, but ended up staring at the annoying little arrow circling around and around, waiting for a page to load.

The signals from our cameras were more clear, so we had a view of the cluttered attic and the office with its windows, plus some downstairs spots like the museum.

"I'll run a quick analysis on the audio records, check for activity spikes," Stacey said. "The ambient wildlife noise isn't doing us any favors with the automated analysis, though. Lots of false positives."

I nodded. The owls were loud outside, but not a thing was stirring inside, not even in the attic. The deflated ball and the badly hand-made car remained still, along with all the other junk.

Stacey checked her audio anomalies, but after a while it seemed every jolt of activity was another owl or coyote.

"I'm going into their office," I said, packing up my laptop. "The WiFi's too spotty out here. Wait out here."

"But Allison said she heard things in there when she was alone."

"Right. Hopefully something will show up to haunt me."

"Be careful."

"Don't worry. I've got The Old Kentucky Boys Bluegrass Gospel on tap. Mountain music for the mountain ghosts."

"Okay." She looked doubtful as she watched me step down from the van.

The lodge certainly didn't feel any more welcoming than it had before. The skin on the back of my neck already crawled as I stepped up onto the porch, into the shadows of its low roof. Before opening the door, I steeled myself with an extra-deep calming breath like they teach in yoga. Well, it was meant to be a calming breath, but I wouldn't say it worked all that well.

I pushed open the door and stepped into the lodge.

In the main room, decades of fireplace smoke had baked into the walls, leaving a permanent aroma of charred wood. The wall of photographs showed a hundred or more moments spanning the history of the camp.

My footsteps sounded loud in my ears as I walked down the side hall and into the office. Our cameras watched patiently, unblinking, as cold mountain breezes rustled the heavy canvas curtains around the huge windows.

I dropped into Allison's chair; the neatness of her desk made it easy to borrow. Josh's desk was chaotic with odds and ends and some model Italian sports cars for added clutter, so I would have needed to clear room for my computer.

Facing the open windows, I searched local newspaper databases. I wasn't surprised to learn the online archives only reached back a few decades. That's typical, especially for smaller local papers. I was lucky to find any digital archives at all.

The easiest articles to find were the most recent, only months old. A typical one described in a giddy tone how "historic treasure" Camp Stony Owl would once again open, "gathering a new generation of campers into its feathery wings."

The article showed Josh and Allison's family in a black and white version of the framed picture on her desk. It read like a barely modified press release; very likely Josh or Allison had written most of it, and the papers had simply run it.

"Camp Stony Owl is the kind of place that young people need today more than ever," one paper quoted Josh. "In this environment, with their feet on the ground and their eyes on the natural world instead of a screen, their hands busy climbing and building and making, they can find the missing parts of themselves. Those parts of ourselves that are often lost in today's world, and so hard to get back."

The article gushed about the family's restoration efforts and their plans to open in the beginning of summer. Nothing new to me.

What I really wanted was some deeper history, but the article brushed over that very lightly: "The campground has been closed for many years, its mysterious ancient stone owl left neglected and overgrown. The Conners' efforts promise to bring new life to this impressive and fascinating site."

Digging deeper took a while. While the twenty-first-century editions were easily searchable online, records from the 1990s and earlier were just image scans and not quite so easy to search. Even those did not extend as far back as the camp's long history.

Each time the curtain rustled or the lodge's timbers creaked, I looked up, half-expecting to see a shape in the large window. I'd kept the curtains open to the night outside, presenting myself as a target to any local entities in search of one.

Something thumped upstairs, directly above my head.

"Stacey, see anything up there?" I whispered via my headset.

"I see no evil, I hear no evil," she said. "Fingers crossed

for a return of last night's cold front from beyond the grave."

"Anything turn up on your audio analysis of what we missed tonight?"

"Oh, yeah. A whole chorus of ghosts chanting 'Wheeeeere is my booooooody? Wheeeeeeeeere is my boooooooody—'"

"Seriously?"

"No, I'm just saying, I would have mentioned that first," Stacey said. "Nothing so far. I'll keep searching."

"Me too. Some of these old newspapers are conveniently stored in blurry PDFs that default to weird sizes. I've found nothing so far. Let me know if anything starts creeping around the lodge."

"You got it, Sarge. Over and out. End of transmission. One and done."

I continued working at my laptop. As the hour grew later, I felt more and more like I was being watched, but Stacey reported nothing. I kept looking through the windows at the porch beyond, the outlines of its supports and banister barely visible in the gloom. Someone or something could have been standing out there, not far away, watching.

The power of suggestion could have been playing a role, of course, after I'd heard Allison's story. For that matter, being alone in that lodge at night would have been creepy under the best of circumstances.

After a lot of searching in the archives, I found something huge.

"Stacey," I said, "listen to this. Thirty-three years ago, three kids died right here at the camp."

She gasped. "No way."

"Yes way. It says they snuck out at night and went paddling in a canoe. No life vests. There was a storm. They drowned. The camp immediately closed. And it looks like it stayed closed ever since."

"Uh, whoa. You'd think somebody would have mentioned that to us," Stacey said.

"Yeah." I grabbed my pocket notebook and started jotting details. The three kids had been fourteen to fifteen years old.

"Why would teenage boys go out on a boat in a storm?" Stacey wondered. "Well, now that I say it aloud, it kinda answers itself."

I nodded, not that she could see it. "Maybe they were out to prove they were tough. Or maybe more was involved. We need to find out everything."

"The poor kids," Stacey said. "Imagine their parents. Send them off for a week at summer camp and never see them again. Ellie, I'm seeing a cold spot forming upstairs."

Even as she spoke, a scraping and rattling sounded from the ceiling like something was being dragged across the attic floorboards.

"What is that?"

"Looks like a... roller skate?" Stacey said. "Um, I think something's about to—"

A loud crash sounded, followed by scattered thuds in its wake.

"That whole table of old sports equipment got turned over," Stacey told me.

I leaped to my feet, my hand on my holstered flashlight. My gaze flicked from the ceiling to the open windows nearby. "What's happening now?"

"There's a couple things still moving. A baseball and a

bat. The bat's just about stopped, but the baseball's rolled off into a corner. And that cold front is back, it's everywhere like a fog, floating through, it's—no. It's gone completely."

"That was fast," I said.

A heavy footfall sounded on the porch outside. I stiffened, watching the nearest of the two big windows, listening intently for the sound of another shoe to drop.

After waiting for what felt like several long, slow years, I finally whispered, "Did you hear that?"

"Huh? Which thing?"

"The porch down here."

"No, I haven't really been focusing on the downstairs, sorry. What happened?"

"I thought I heard... something." The curtains swayed in the outdoor breeze; it was easy to imagine someone standing just out of sight out there, listening to me, perhaps watching from the shadows. I'd only heard the one footstep, but it had been loud and clear, like the clomp of a heavy boot.

I couldn't bring myself to say the word *footstep* to Stacey, though, or tell her that I felt like someone was out there. It was as if saying it would cause the unseen entity to spring into action, to attack me while I was alone.

Trembling, I closed my laptop and turned off the desk lamp, extinguishing all the light in the room. This made it easier for me to watch the gloom outside the windows for any odd shapes or movement. It also made me feel less like I was on a lighted stage, fully visible to anyone stalking around outside.

"Are you *sure* you don't see anything down here?" I whispered, hoping she caught my urgent tone.

"Downstairs? Nope. Sorry."

I approached the windows cautiously. The heavy canvas curtains shifted in the wind. I could feel the chilled air move across my skin, smell the damp green of the forest. The calling of the owls picked up. *Hoo h-hoo, hoo h-hoo.*

"The owls must have gotten into the peanut butter, because they are acting nutty," Stacey whispered in my ear. She would have been watching through the cameras behind me, seeing me in shades of green on the night vision, probably yellow and orange on the thermal.

I leaned closer to the window where I'd heard the single footstep and peered out into the moonlit night. The central hub of the big fire pit was easy to see, as any overhanging limbs had been wisely cleared away to leave a clear path to the open sky. A few blackened logs lay there, left from the Conners' last fire.

The porch itself was much darker, hooded by its low roof.

It was hard to make myself speak, to intentionally draw the attention of whoever or whatever might be out there.

"H-hello?" I hated the shakiness and hesitation in my voice. I cleared my throat and tried again, a little bolder: "Is someone there? Show yourself." That second part took some effort, because I wasn't sure I was mentally ready at that moment to see some dead thing stepping out at me, even if it meant progress on the case.

I leaned closer to the window screen until my face was against the cold metal mesh. I looked to the left, saw nothing but floorboards and an old rocking chair. Then I looked to the right. Nothing again, just some firewood stacked under the shelter of the back porch.

With a sigh, I stepped back. "I guess it was nothing.

Anything upstairs?"

"Not since the cold front vanished like my mom's dog when you pull out the vacuum cleaner."

Another floorboard creaked. Behind me, inside the room somewhere.

"Did you hear that?" Stacey whispered.

I turned toward the sound, bracing myself for whatever might be standing there.

Across the room, a shape moved in the doorway. It was gone as soon as I saw it, like someone had just walked past and out of sight down the hall.

"There *is* someone here," I whispered. I hurried to the door, drawing my flashlight but keeping it off.

"Want me to come in?"

"Stand by and keep watch." Drawing a deep breath, I stepped into the hall.

There was nothing to see, either in the hallway or in what I could discern of the main fireplace room up ahead. Moving up the hall, I looked into the open door to a small classroom with microscopes, test tubes, and ecology posters. Nobody was there.

The big fireplace room was shadowy and dim, lit only by moonlight, quiet and still.

I debated whether to head back to the office or go check the museum area, but then Stacey's voice broke in: "Ellie, something's upstairs."

"Something like what?"

"It looked like a person, but it just cut the corner of the night vision camera. It was heading toward that cabin-type area with the bedroom and bathroom inside."

"I'll check it out. Could be the one I was just following."

"I'm coming with you."

I should have protested, because the dead are more likely to appear to one person than to two, but this campground made me feel more uneasy than the average haunted house. Perhaps there had been a lot of tragedy or violence here. Maybe it was the stony owl that made the difference, an ancient burial ground that had been disturbed, just the kind of thing that could give an environment a deep and powerful negative psychic charge —a curse, in effect.

But that was just one possibility. The stony owl could be entirely benign; any souls associated with it should have moved on centuries earlier. However, any spirit that *had* clung to the earthly plane that long was likely to be a twisted and dangerous type, in my experience.

On the other hand, maybe the campground was haunted by the deaths of the three boys I'd read about. Were they still hanging around the campground? Kicking around sports equipment in the attic, perhaps? Playing hide and seek with Shiloh?

The front door creaked open. Stacey entered, armed with a video camera. "Ready to capture these ghosts, ma'am. Well, images of them. Then the real thing. Unless there's a way to skip ahead."

"I wish we could."

We walked through the folding doors at the back of the utility closet, past a shiny new water heater, and up the narrow stairs to the second floor.

"I haven't been this nervous going into an attic since playing Postman at Baird Scott's party in tenth grade," Stacey whispered.

"Shh." I cut her off, partly so we could approach the

entity in silence, partly because I was worried she would continue her story with more details.

At the top of the stairs, I brought out my EMF meter, a handy little doodad that helps identify any spikes in electromagnetic activity or drops in temperature.

We walked among the spilled sports equipment, Stacey recording video while I gathered EMF readings.

"They should just toss half this junk," Stacey whispered. "And maybe the other half, too."

The electromagnetic readings rose around the baseball and bat, possibly indicating some residual psychokinetic energy from whatever had knocked them over.

"It was moving that way." Stacey pointed to the closed door of the indoor cabin dominating the back corner.

"Maybe there's still a resident in that old room."

"And now we have to go poking around in it."

"Feel free to wait here." I started toward the door, taking readings.

"Forget that. I'm with you." Stacey stayed close behind, watching me through her compact video camera.

Near the closed door, the EMF meter lit up. Stacey's gasp told me she'd seen it.

I touched the iron door handle.

"It's cold," I whispered, then opened it. I yanked my hand off the handle and waved it vigorously to shake off the cold, as though I were greeting whatever entity awaited us.

There was nothing obvious inside the bedroom of the indoor cabin, no sign of the walking apparition that Stacey and I had glimpsed. My EMF meter was lit up and flashing like a Christmas tree, though, and the room was noticeably colder even though its windows were shuttered.

"The ambient temperature in here is ten degrees lower than the rest of the attic." I led the way through the clutter of boxes, past the mildewed heap of an old tennis net, following the EMF readings. I squeezed past the bed, barely visible under a crumpled tarp, rusty paint buckets, and old boxes.

Like the bread crumbs in Hansel and Gretel, the EMF spikes and temperature drops led inexorably to the dark, windowless bathroom in the corner. I would have preferred a candy house, personally.

Leaving the light off, I stepped inside. There was barely enough room to turn around; dusty cardboard boxes were heaped in the bathtub. Hooks, lures, and a coil of fishing line lay in the sink.

"Anybody here?" My voice echoed back in the small chamber. I caught movement at the corner of my eye. Turning quickly to look, I faced my own reflection looking back at me from the medicine cabinet mirror over the sink.

Stacey opened her mouth to say something, but I motioned for her to stay quiet. I followed my own advice and went as still and silent as I could manage, watching and listening.

"I'm not seeing anything," Stacey finally said anyway, still looking at her camera display.

"The temperature's almost back to normal. The EMF spikes have stopped, too. Whatever we followed in here, it's gone now." I looked over minute cracks in the unadorned plaster wall, as if I'd find some sort of ghost-goo left behind.

"Maybe it just came by to brush its teeth before heading out," Stacey said.

I swung open the medicine cabinet and looked over the

narrow steel shelves. A few items were inside, neatly arranged as if for inspection by a drill sergeant.

"Look at this." I eased aside so she could bring the camera closer. It was a tight fit with both of us in the room. "A can of hair pomade. A straight razor, with a rotten leather strop for sharpening."

"It's like stuff my grandpa's grandpa would have used."

Carefully, I lifted the straight razor and swung it open. The blade was dull and rusty.

"I hope you brought tetanus shots, Ellie," Stacey said, in a warning tone.

I gently replaced the blade. "Okay. I don't know about you, but I'm about ready to get out of here—"

"So ready. My bags are packed. Not, you know, literally. But up here." She tapped her head. "I'm all packed and ready to go. Mentally."

"Great." I continued to take readings as we made our way back to the stairs.

Before we left, I took a long look at the items scattered on the floor—the baseball bat, the deflated rubber ball, the lumpy wooden toy car that looked like it wouldn't have rolled very fast down even the steepest and greasiest of hills.

"What do you think?" Stacey asked me, waiting halfway down the steps.

"I think there's a good chance this place has a serious paranormal infestation," I said. "Maybe it's those three kids, maybe it's something else. Whatever it is has enough psychokinetic power to bump objects around. And if it can move an object—"

"It can hurt somebody," Stacey finished.

I nodded, and we moved on, not feeling at all uplifted

by what we'd encountered so far. And there was still a long night ahead.

Chapter Fourteen

We returned to the van, where I popped open a cold canned coffee—not my favorite thing, but better than the carbonated herbal energy drinks Stacey brings, at least in my opinion.

"It's like a weight lifted off our backs the moment we came outside, huh?" Stacey said, between sips of something loaded with ginseng and guarana. "It's pretty wrong in there."

"Yeah, I can't say I'm in favor of them opening this place for kids," I said.

"It'll be safe by the time we're done with it, though."

"Not necessarily." I let that hang in the air. We hadn't cracked every case, hadn't successfully purged the troublesome spirits at every turn. There had been cases where we couldn't help, or where the client had grown impatient and fired us. Josh was threatening to do exactly that, in his sales-friendly way.

I drove out of the parking lot and down the rutted gravel utility road, driving slowly so I wouldn't make a lot of noise approaching the caretaker's cottage where the Conners lived. We planned to keep our distance from the house, but we needed to get around the hill a little bit, close enough to receive clear signals from our cameras inside.

As we rounded the last bend to their house, I cut the headlights so they wouldn't blare through anyone's bedroom window. I parked in the road, still a few dozen yards from the house, and killed the engine.

The house was dark, much of its shape cloaked by the woods that had grown in close around it. Everyone was likely asleep; it was nearly three in the morning.

"Okay, let's see what we've got." Stacey pulled the feeds from the cameras and microphone hidden in Allison and Josh's room.

Sitting in the back of the van with Stacey, I watched the monitors come online. We looked at thermal and night vision images of Allison and Josh lying in bed, which definitely felt intrusive on our part. It would have helped if Josh had worn a shirt.

"Josh doesn't look like he misses many days at the gym." Stacey gestured at the night vision image of his muscular arm.

"That's inappropriate."

"But accurate. I mean, maybe he skips leg day occasionally—"

"We're supposed to be focused on the windows."

"I am, but nothing's happening. Do you think the tall shadow figure that walked through their room is the same one we saw at the lodge?"

"No idea."

"If it's not, this place is starting to seem overrun with ghosts."

"Yep. There's certainly space for them." I looked ahead through the windshield at the dense, gloomy woods that surrounded the house and engulfed the hillside trails winding toward the ancient effigy above. "Space and time."

Despite Stacey's comment, the house didn't seem overrun with ghosts at the moment. Josh and Allison slept peacefully. We couldn't see the rest of the house's interior. The microphone under their bed was large and sensitive enough to pick up the soft sound of Allison's breathing; if there was a noise anywhere in the house, we'd probably hear it.

Nearly an hour passed before I glimpsed something move—not on the monitor, but up ahead, in the woods. I grabbed night vision goggles and scrambled toward the front of the van to look out the windshield.

"What's up?" Stacey asked.

"Maybe nothing." Sliding on the heavy goggles, I tried for a better look at the moving shape.

There it was—a roughly human-sized form weaving through the woods, sometimes visible and sometimes not, but definitely heading right for our clients' house. It could have come from the lake and the small village of activity huts there... or it could have come down from the hilltop.

"It's not nothing," I said. "I'll check it out."

"Should I come?"

I shook my head. "We may have chased away the entity at the lodge. I'll get a better chance at a closer look if I go alone."

"The Rule of One," Stacey intoned, with great

solemnity, though I don't think we'd ever used that term before. It made sense, though—ghosts are most likely to show up when a living person is alone, will sometimes show up for two people, but are least likely to appear in front of a group of people. A ghost who does that is typically stirred up and active, very energized. Normally, they avoid the living, keeping to the dark and lonely places of the world where they can suffer in peace.

"Yeah, sure. The Rule of One." I turned off the van's automatic interior light before opening the door and stepping down onto the dirt road. I closed the door behind me as softly as I could, trying to make no noise at all.

I walked along the side of the road, staying under the shadows of the trees. My night vision goggles presented the path ahead in varied shades of green. I carried our smallest night vision camera in case I found anything.

Ahead, I saw no sign of the walker in the woods, but walls of undergrowth blocked my view. It might have gone toward Allison's bedroom, where she'd seen the tall shadow person enter their house.

I picked up the pace, not wanting to miss my chance to encounter the entity before it walked indoors or vanished back into the forest.

As I drew closer, approaching the clients' parked cars, a pale shape emerged from among the trees, moving rapidly in my direction. It was human-shaped and very solid. Either it was a very strong apparition or an actual live human out here in the predawn.

I stopped next to Allison's SUV, awkwardly trying to hide out of sight, but not trying to look like I was hiding in case I'd already been spotted.

Footsteps approached, solid and regular. They crossed

in front of the car that I hid behind.

I held my breath as the footsteps came near. Definitely a living person, not a ghost. Yikes.

The footsteps walked right past where I hid, crossing in front of the car instead of behind it.

I leaned out from behind the car and saw the figure more clearly as it approached the front door of the cottage. It was male, shirtless and muscular; for a moment I took it for Josh, but then I remembered I'd just seen him in his own bed.

Nate, I realized. This was confirmed when he glanced around nervously, as if he sensed someone watching him, and I finally got a halfway decent look at his face.

I froze where I was; moving was more likely to attract his attention than remaining motionless in the shadows.

He wasn't looking at me, though, but at our van up the road, visible in the thin moonlight if one's eyes were sharp enough. Apparently his were.

Nate strode right up between the cars, toward the van and toward me. I backed out of the way, but there was nowhere to hide.

He spotted me and jumped back. The space alien pilot look of my night vision goggles probably didn't help.

"Hey, there," I said, as though the two of us running into each other in the driveway at four in the morning was a completely normal, everyday occurrence. I raised my goggles to reduce my alien invader look a bit. "What's up?"

"What..." He looked from me to the van. "What's going on?"

This was a perfectly reasonable question on his part, one I was forbidden by his parents to answer truthfully. And if you can't tell the truth and you can't stay silent, then you don't have much choice left but to come up with a lie. Fast.

"Um, this is embarrassing," I began, which bought me a few extra seconds. No lies so far. But then I continued, "We were hoping to get some sunrise footage of the owl."

"The owl?"

"Yeah, the way its eyes change with the position of the sun. I think it might have been an intentional feature by the original creators."

"Okay." He sounded instantly bored by this. "Where's Stacey?"

"Back in the van."

"You missed a trailhead back there. The hill has a couple. That one's pretty overgrown, though. The one behind our house is longer but easier. The wild animals use it."

"There's a trail in the woods behind your house? By your parents' room?"

"Kind of a deer path, yeah. Sometimes you see a rabbit or fox there." He yawned. Now that my eyes had adjusted from night vision to moonlight, I could see how tired he looked. "I have to get inside before my parents wake up. But yeah, I'll take you up that way. And maybe don't tell my parents I was out here."

"Why not?" I asked. "Were you doing something exciting and fun?"

"Sometimes I just want to go for a walk." His tone was irritated, but to be fair, my question had been nosy. "Get away from everyone. Get out and admire, you know, nature. The natureness of it all." That last part didn't sound remotely sincere to me. I didn't see Nate wandering out in the wee hours of the morning to write sonnets about stars and moonlight. Ephraim, maybe. Or maybe I didn't know these kids as well as I thought. "But my mom will freak out. Like where am I going to go? A party? We're in the middle of nowhere. I couldn't get into trouble if I wanted to. Which I don't, because colleges look at that."

"Maybe she's worried about you getting hurt. They think a black bear or another large animal did some damage around the camp. The cabin. The lodge, before you moved in."

"Black bears are the smallest and weakest of all bears. And we've never even seen one, so if there is one, then it's avoiding people."

"What about mountain lions?" I said.

"This isn't *Where the Red Fern Grows*. Which was a lame movie, I'm never watching that again. These woods are tame. They're modern. There's nothing I can't handle out here. But still, don't tell my parents. All right? My dad wouldn't care, but my mom's always freaking out lately. And Ephraim's a perma-freak, but that's a whole 'nother problem in my life. We cool?"

"I guess I can agree to that, for now, if you promise to be careful." I thought of the boys who'd drowned. "And stay away from the lake. Don't ever go there alone."

"Yeah, yeah, standard buddy system stuff. I've got the Lifesaving merit badge." He yawned and stretched, looking uphill toward the van. "Tell Stacey I said what's up."

"Sure. Good night, Nathan."

"Just Nate." He trudged back to the front door and let himself inside, treading lightly, disturbing none of the porch floorboards, as if he were no stranger to sneaking in and out at night.

"That was super odd," Stacey said over the headset.

"What do you think he was doing?"

"Maybe he's telling the truth." I started back up the road to rejoin Stacey.

"Or maybe he doesn't like being inside that house at night," Stacey said. "Maybe he saw something."

"You work on talking to him. He likes you." I turned off the headset and climbed into the van with her.

"Are you sure we shouldn't tell his parents we saw him out late?"

"I'm not sure, no. But if he's holding something back from us, then ratting him out to his parents is not the quickest way to gain his trust so he opens up. And he has a point—there's a limit to how much trouble a kid can get in around here. He's literally a Boy Scout. I told him to stay away from the lake. He wasn't wet, so he wasn't swimming."

"He could have been out paddling. Alone."

"Let's hope not," I said. "He seemed to understand the buddy system."

A little while later, after a complicated process of turning the van around on the dirt road without shining my headlights into the house, I drove us back to the lodge.

We hiked down the trail together, keeping close, our flashlight beams carving away some of the darkness ahead. Owls screeched above.

"What's that sound?" Stacey asked as we finally approached the boys' cabin circle where our borrowed bunks awaited. I was so tired that the simple shelter with its bunk beds was going to feel as luxurious as a Four Seasons suite.

I stopped. Something thudded in the distance. Again. And again, banging at regular intervals.

"It's that door to Bobcat Cabin," I said.

"I thought we secured that."

"We did. And we have all that equipment inside."

Stacey's eyes widened; we were both thinking of the damage done by the alleged invisible black bear, which was very possibly not a bear at all but the invisible laughing entity that had taunted me in there. The entity had knocked around Josh's tools, and our cameras were not cheap.

We both ran the rest of the way down the trail to the cabins.

Chapter Fifteen

The door to Bobcat Cabin repeatedly banged against the outer wall of the cabin, slammed by the wind. Each time the door opened, it would creak shut again, perhaps pulled by the force of gravity and guided by the warp of the doorframe. Then the wind would pick up and blow the door open once more.

"We'd better have a look inside," I said, though I felt apprehensive. I was already worn down and didn't feel like chasing the invisible giggler again. "Let's make it quick. Keep your ears open."

We stepped inside, and I wasn't shy about jabbing the beam of my flashlight into dark corners.

No giggling arose as we walked into the first bedroom. The place was as quiet as it was dark.

The bunks had moved around, though, pushed out from the walls at odd angles to each other. Whatever had moved the bunks had also moved—

"The camera!" Stacey ran toward the knocked-over tripod and hurriedly inspected the night vision camera. "The lens is fine. Battery's drained, though."

"Hopefully it recorded whatever knocked it over."

The audio recorder with its delicate microphone was drained, too. We collected that along with the camera. I kept an eye on the closet, on guard for anything to emerge from among the broken shelves and the gaping hole in the back wall.

We eventually made our way to the other bedroom. Nothing had changed there, as far as we could tell. Our thermal camera remained perched atop its tripod, though its battery was drained, too.

"The giggler must have been hungry," I murmured. "I hate when they feed on our electricity."

As we trudged back to Wolf Cabin, our home base, I had every intention of powering up the gear and finding any secrets we might have collected. Once we got there, the first thing we did was set the batteries to recharge.

Recharging would take a while, though. When my boots were off, stretching out on the bunk seemed like a great idea. The reassurance of sunlight would come before long.

I slept uneasily, with flickering dreams where strange laughter echoed and shadowy children chased me among a maze of cabins and bonfires.

Pushing open a rickety, creaking door, I found my way outside. A campfire blazed nearby, filling the air with the smell of fire, a smell I hated.

I staggered forward, up along a steep, narrow trail through the woods.

Glancing back, I saw the strange maze I'd emerged

from had been reduced to a single crumbling, skeletal cabin, overgrown and nearly consumed by the foggy woods around it. All the light and heat of the fire was gone.

Softly, as though from a distance, I could hear laughter through the cabin's open doorway. The shadow children, the ones who'd been chasing me.

The door to the cabin, clinging by two of its three hinges, slammed shut with a rusty squeal and locked itself from within, cutting off their voices.

I turned to look uphill. The path was steep and incredibly long, making me think of Machu Picchu or the ziggurats of ancient Mesopotamia—long, stone stairways to heaven connecting humans below to the gods above. The symbolism was always clear, across continents and centuries, with hardly a word needing to be said to explain it.

Up there, I know, was the great stone owl, and a presence that waited. A presence that had silenced the laughing children. A presence that knew I was here.

I shivered. The fear twisted my stomach into knots. Whatever was up there, I didn't want to face it.

Something grabbed me—a claw-like tree branch, reaching out from the forest, seizing my arm, trapping me.

It began to shake me. A knothole in the tree opened and said my name.

I awoke on my bunk. The grip on my arm was still there. Slender but strong fingers, digging at me, shaking me.

"Ellie?" Stacey leaned over me. Her face had replaced the knothole. "Are you up?"

"Huh?" I took a moment to sort out where I was—in the cabin, with daylight gushing in through the window.

"Looked like you were having a bad dream," she said. "Lots of grunting and twisting and turning."

"Yeah." I sat up and stretched. "Just your basic *Children of the Corn* nightmare scenario. Shadow children chasing me toward He Who Walks Behind the Campfire. How'd you sleep?"

"Bad dreams, too. Look at this." She pressed a tablet into my hands. A video clip was set up, currently paused.

The sight of it jolted me awake like a shot of espresso. Well, maybe not quite that well, but it snapped me out of my dreamy state. "That's from inside the cabin?"

"Yep. The last few seconds before it went dead." Stacey reached over and touched the *play* triangle.

The bunk beds and closet appeared in night vision green. At first, everything was still in the quiet, empty room.

Then one set of bunk beds slid several inches across the floor, as if someone had pushed one corner of it. It stopped as abruptly as it had begun.

"Did you see it?" Stacey asked.

"Yeah, of course."

"Now look." As she pointed, the other bunk bed moved several inches from the wall, too, shoved by an invisible force. This knocked over the camera tripod, and the video ended.

"Wow. Good job, Stacey." I rubbed my eyes. "Did you correlate it with—"

"Yep." She played another video clip, this one from the thermal in the cabin's other bedroom, which I'd pointed right at the wrecked closet.

A cold spot emerged from the closet, then grew. And grew. And grew. It was like a cold fog, expanding to fill the room.

"Where have we seen that before?" I asked, fairly rhetorically.

"Upstairs in the lodge. It looks like the same entity."

"It could be a cluster of them," I said.

"The three boys?"

"Maybe. But we've only scratched the surface of this place's history. Did you also check the—"

"Of course I checked the audio, and yes, we caught something." She tapped a button on her laptop.

A high-pitched shrieking laugh filled the room, climbing in volume for a couple of seconds before ending abruptly.

"The invisible giggler," I muttered.

"So the huge cold spot is also the giggler," Stacey said. "Assuming it's the same huge cold spot from the lodge and not a different huge cold spot. And that just leaves the tall guy who walks around with heavy footsteps."

"Which was also seen in two locations. So we *could* be dealing with up to four distinct entities. Or entity clusters. Three people dying together could stick together in death, forming a cluster. Especially if they shared any kind of bond in life."

"Cool. I'll be sure to think about that while using their old shower." Stacey grabbed her backpack, and I reluctantly grabbed my own and went with her to the bathhouse, not far from the haunted Bobcat Cabin. As we stood in the shadowy brick-walled showers, I tried not to let the memory of that invisible laughter play again and again inside my head.

Chapter Sixteen

After the bathhouse, we headed up to the lodge. I texted Allison that I hoped Josh could meet us there, alone.

When he showed up, he looked freshly blow-dried, wearing his usual wide smile and shaking our hands.

"Allison tells me you want to hear more about the camp," he said.

"It would help with our investigation, and we could record it to use for your website. That's probably the bigger value to you," I said.

"The museum area would make a good background," Stacey said.

"Fantastic idea. I like it." Josh double-finger-gunned her before trotting over to the museum. He hadn't asked about our overnight observation, so I held back on mentioning the strange events in the cabin. There was no telling how he might react, and I wanted him relaxed and chatty.

Stacey took over, posing him in front of the display about the Stony Owl effigy. It included an aerial photo, quartzite stones taken from the mound and arranged in a miniature imitation of the original, and a number of excavated tools, weapons, and pottery shards.

"You want to turn about three-quarters of the way toward me," Stacey said. She'd set up a couple of portable lights from the van for a better video. "Yep, that's it. Looks good. Let me know when you're ready."

"So, where do I begin?" Josh suddenly looked nervous, his smile slipping.

"Imagine someone's never heard of this place," I said. "How would you tell them about the owl?"

He thought it over and nodded. "Okay. I'm ready. Action!"

"Hey, *I* say 'action,'" Stacey told him. "Action!"

Josh began. He did little more than read the little signs in the display, but he did so with great zeal, pointing out the arrowheads and beads, the obsidian knife and ax head, the plate of copper with the owl etching. "They say Stony Owl could be thousands of years old," he said after a while. "No one knows for sure. What we know is that, to the people who lived way, way back then, it was a place of great importance. And we are proud to carry on that tradition today, maintaining the site as a valuable cultural resource for our campers. The great old Stony Owl teaches us to back up and take the long view, the big picture, and really consider what's important in life. What's really going to last, and what will matter in the long run."

"Oh, that's great!" Stacey said. "Can you tell us what we do know about its history?"

"We don't know much about who built the owl, or why. Our modern understanding begins with Charles Tennyford." He pointed to the 1896 photograph of a bearded man in a straw hat. "Kind of a Renaissance man and treasure hunter. Farmer, amateur chemist, inventor, though not of anything that really caught on. He led the excavation of the site. Trees had to be felled and undergrowth hacked through. The forest had grown thick over the centuries.

"They dug a trench through the owl." He indicated another photograph. A small digging crew had gouged a long furrow into the owl's side, like a deep stab wound all the way to its heart. "They moved more than a ton of rocks, one shovel at a time, to unearth the artifacts you see here."

"And he found human remains?" I asked.

"Yeah..." Josh looked at the photograph tucked down in a bottom corner, showing the bearded Tennyford in his straw hat holding up the skull and beads. "We should probably take that picture out. I don't think I have the key." He patted his pocket and shook his head. "Probably in the office."

"Were the bones returned to the grave?" I asked.

"I would think so. They're not here. This shouldn't go into the promotional video. I'm taking that picture out, okay? It seems insensitive, you know, by today's standards."

"Did Tennyford leave any records we can look at? Notes?" I asked.

Josh shrugged. "It wouldn't be here. The camp wasn't built until decades later. I think he published an article about it somewhere. I know he thought the old walls lining the trails might have been the ruins of some ancient military defense, and maybe there was a battle here a long time ago."

"Did he find any evidence of that?"

"Not that I know of. I don't know much about him beyond what's here." He gestured at the museum display. "This is where I learned about him."

He shifted over to the plant and wildlife display, which would make good website fodder and seemed to genuinely interest Stacey. I ignored them, staring at the old artifacts instead, wondering if an old native burial site was really the best place for a kids' summer camp.

In the main room, Stacey had Josh stand at the wall of photographs. He seemed on firmer footing, grinning wide and gesturing expansively, like he was about to explain the timeshare condo deal of a lifetime.

"Camp Stony Owl was first opened in 1920 by Reverend Roger Carmody and his wife Laurie Ann." Josh pointed to the black and white picture of the founders. Carmody had a sharp nose and a serious, somber look. Where he was tall and burly, and had the rigid bearing of a military man, his wife Laurie Ann was short and plump with a cheerful smile, her arms draped affectionately around two college-aged counselors, one male and one female.

They stood before a campfire, flanked by campers, everyone in matching uniforms and wide-brimmed campaign hats. "The camp grew year by year, with campers coming from all around. It closed during the Great Depression but eventually reopened in the 1970s. Generations of children have been happy to call Camp Stony Owl their summer home, a place where they come for adventure and leave with a lifetime of treasured memories." He paused and remained completely still, like he was expecting her to say *cut*.

"And you came here as a kid yourself, right?" I asked.

"Well, uh, yeah." He stumbled over his words before recovering. "That's why I know what a special place this is. I wanted to bring back all of that old magic for today's kids. My own kids most of all."

"And has it?" I asked.

"Has it what?"

"Brought back the magic for your family?"

He scowled and dropped out of character, his tone clearly annoyed. "What kind of question is that?"

"Oh, sorry," I said, feigning more remorse than I felt. "I thought it was kind of a softball question."

"Right." He rubbed his head. "Sorry. Can we cut it?"

"Of course," Stacey said, beaming at him to try to cheer him up.

"My family has... enjoyed the challenge of... let's skip ahead to something else." He seemed rattled, less focused now. "What should we talk about next? Our programs and activities? A day in the life of a Stony Owl camper? We can start at the ropes course, that was always my favorite."

"Why did it close?" I asked.

"Sorry?"

"Why did the camp close last time? You said it was the Great Depression the first time."

"Right." He stared at the camera like a deer who'd wandered into a whole stadium full of bright lights. "Can we stop for a second?"

"Of course." Stacey paused the recording.

"We really don't need to get into all that depressing stuff," Josh said.

"What do you mean?" I asked, doing my level best to sound innocent of any knowledge about drowned kids.

"The reason it closed before." He licked his lips and shook his head. "It wasn't the camp's fault. They brought it on themselves."

"Who did?" That was me, trying even harder to sound unaware.

"The guys. Paul and Thomas. And Kyle. They snuck out at night when the weather was bad. They didn't even use vests." He shook his head. "It wasn't fair to close the camp over it. They broke the rules. All of them, maybe."

"And that led to the camp closing?"

"Of course." He looked at me like I was crazy. "Three campers died. Never mind whose fault it was, or how they risked their lives just to..." He shook his head.

"To what?"

"To see how tough they were, I guess." Josh looked away. "Anyway, the camp shouldn't have been closed, that's how I felt. Not permanently. Obviously, we'll implement stricter, more modern safety precautions. But at some point people are responsible for their own choices. You can't help it if other people insist on doing something dangerous. Right?"

"Of course," I said, thinking that he was desperately seeking some validation on that. "Did you know the boys who drowned?"

"We were here at the same time. We don't need to talk about this for the website."

"It's not for the website."

"Of course." He finally looked me in the eyes again. "Are you going to say they're haunting the campground?"

"Well—"

"Because that is really, and I don't say this lightly, in very poor taste. It's one thing to tell legends of ancient spirits walking the trails. The Trailwalker legend, that's a part of this place, and it's a fun campfire story. But those boys were real. They had families. And friends. You can hurt people like this."

"We're not trying to hurt anyone," I said. "We recorded more activity last night. We don't know what's causing it, but the more we learn about the history of the place, the sooner we can identify and resolve the problems—"

"The only problem here is that my family doesn't want to adapt to changes," he said. "My kids are screen zombies. My wife likes a high level of creature comforts. Calling this campground haunted is just Allison's latest reason for not liking it."

"Haunted?" The new voice was Ephraim, looking at us through a window by the lodge's front door. The window was open, and he'd heard us through the screen. He walked in through the front door, his ragged clothes dotted with white paint. "Mom thinks the campground's haunted?"

Josh jumped, at a loss for words, and gave Stacey and me an imploring look.

We held our tongues, doing our best not to step into the middle of any family problems.

"She doesn't *really* think it's haunted, champ," Josh said. "We're just trying to set her mind at ease."

"So what did you record?" Ephraim asked me. "Last night?"

Now I was at a loss for words. "Well...ah...you see..."

"Because I've kinda seen some weird stuff, too," Ephraim said. "Like in our house. One time I saw this guy walking, only not a guy, because it's too tall. And branches at the top, like a tree, only it's really just a shadow, and I think I saw it this other time in the woods behind our house, on that deer path from Stony Owl Hill—"

"Enough!" Josh said. "Fine. Let's see what you have."

"Our recordings?" I asked.

"Yep." Josh sank down on a patched old sofa. "Convince me. Let's see what we're paying for."

I hesitated, not sure if we should risk scaring Ephraim. But if he'd already been seeing things, maybe we could reassure him he wasn't alone with the problem.

Stacey raised her eyebrows at me in a questioning way.

"Go ahead," I told her.

Soon the two of them stared at Stacey's laptop on the scratched thrift-store coffee table. She showed them the beds sliding briefly across the floor, knocking over the camera. Ephraim's mouth dropped open. Josh shook his head.

"Someone could have moved those from off camera," Josh said.

"But we didn't," I told him. "We weren't even in that cabin when this happened."

"So why did you record some empty cabin in the middle of the night, anyway?" Ephraim asked.

I looked at Josh, letting him decide on the answer.

"These ladies kind of specialize in looking for, uh, well." Josh made a meaningless gesture with one hand while avoiding eye contact with his son.

"Things that go bump in the night," Stacey said.

"Oh. Seriously?" Ephraim's face showed confusion, then dawning interest, looking at me in a new way. "You're paranormal investigators?"

"We are," I said.

"And Mom hired them?" Ephraim looked at Josh, who nodded. "Wow. I thought I was the only one. This place really is all freaked up, isn't it?"

"Watch your language," Josh said.

"I did, though."

"The microphone picked this up at the same time." Stacey replayed the moving-bed clip with the screech of laughter added.

Josh flinched as if someone had punched him.

"That's crazy," Ephraim said, shuddering.

"What have you experienced here, Ephraim?" I asked.

"Just like I said." He glanced uncomfortably at his father. "That tall shape."

"You said something like a tree."

"Yeah. Taller than a person, branches all over the top." He glanced at his father again. "I'm not making it up."

Josh looked from Ephraim to us. "You're sure nobody was in the cabin when these beds moved?"

"I am certain that neither of us was in there," I said. "I suppose, technically, we can't say that someone didn't hypothetically sneak in there and knock things around. We do have footage from outside the cabin, though, so we can check that for signs of anyone coming or going."

"But you haven't yet?" Josh asked. "So it could still be a prank."

"There *is* weird stuff happening around here, Dad," Ephraim said.

Josh said nothing, staring at the screen.

"Does Nate know?" Ephraim asked, jarring Josh into movement again.

"No," Josh said, but he looked befuddled, and his response sounded almost reflexive. "Does Nate know what?"

"That the camp is haunted," Ephraim said. "And they're investigating."

"There's no need to tell Nate," Josh said. "You kids will blow things out of proportion. Listen, I know this place is old, and maybe strange things happen sometimes. There is still nothing to worry about. Your mom and I are watching out for you."

"Okay." Ephraim cast a doubtful look at Stacey and me, his two alleged guardians from supernatural evil. "If you say so."

"If there's anything here, we will do our best to get rid of it," I said. "I promise you that. Both of you."

The doubt didn't leave Ephraim's face, but Josh's hardened a bit, maybe a glimmer of resentment there. He put a hand on his pale, gangly son's shoulder and steered him toward the door. "We still have a long list for today," he said. As they walked out, Josh looked back at us. "I think we're done here," he added in a frosty tone before they left.

Stacey and I looked at each other but kept quiet, remembering how Ephraim had overheard us through the window. Their footsteps clomped away down the front porch steps, much like those Allison had heard while working alone at night.

Chapter Seventeen

"Could have gone better," Stacey said. "What's next?"

"Research," I said. "We need to know more about the camp than Josh is willing to tell us."

"You think he's holding out on us, details-wise?" Stacey asked.

"I think it's getting a little personal for him. It was one thing to let us hunt ghosts around his camp, another to talk about people he knew in life, people who died. We may be on the road to getting fired now. But in case we are, we can at least leave Allison with more information than we've dug up so far."

"As long as 'digging up' doesn't refer to an activity we'll be doing up at the old burial mound under a full moon."

"Never fear. You want property records again?"

"Ugh." She rubbed her head. "I want stronger coffee if we're going to do that. Like a fire hose of the midnight black stuff."

"That can be arranged."

We clambered into the van and drove up the old road to the wooden palisade gate.

"Looks like you're the gatekeeper," I told Stacey. "Since I'm the van driver."

She sighed and dropped out of the van, then lifted away the heavy board latch and swung the gate open. After I drove through, she closed it and climbed back in.

"It seems brighter outside the camp, doesn't it?" Stacey asked as we pulled onto the somewhat more civilized blacktop clinging to the mountainside. Nervous sweat rose from my palms, making the steering wheel slippery. Camp Stony Owl was much too high for my taste.

"It's great," I said through gritted teeth, trying to keep my eyes on the road instead of wandering over to the death drop beyond the edge of the road.

It was a half-hour drive to Blairsville, population seven hundred-ish. It was the county's seat and largest town, the place to find the library, government, local newspaper, and even the historical society, all pretty much in walking distance of each other. Convenient. The town offered plenty of restaurants and boutique shops for all the tourists escaping the cities for the mountains.

"We should eat first." Stacey poked at her stomach. "I'm getting pretty growly. Old Josh didn't cook us any waffles this morning. We're obviously on his bad side."

"Research first," I said. "We've only got a few hours before things close down."

"Just don't send me to the property records room at the town hall," Stacey pleaded. "I've done nothing to deserve it."

"We can focus on the library today," I said, having mercy on her.

The library turned out to be a charming little brick building across the street from a grassy knoll of a churchyard full of gravestones. We quickly found our way to the reference section. We discovered the town paper, the *North Georgia News*, had been in print since 1909, but I wanted to look back into the history of the amateur archaeologist Charles Tennyford, who'd excavated the owl years before that.

"Do you want to look at the 1920s in the *North Georgia News* or at the 1890s in the *North Georgia Citizen* of Dalton?" I asked Stacey.

"The 1920s, I guess," she said. "I can read about flappers and Al Capone."

Soon we summoned up, via microfilm, pale articles from the gloomy past.

I started in 1896. The *Citizen* had indeed found the clearing and excavation of the "ancient Indian ritual site" to be of interest:

> The existence of the old mound having long been known to local farmers, great surprise ensued when Tennyford uncovered the site's true shape, a horned and winged figure he christened 'Great Stony Owl.'
>
> "They may have worshiped the owl as a god, as the ancient Greeks revered the owl as the herald of their goddess Athena," said Tennyford. "I believe we may have discovered an ancient idol, hinting at a lost civilization that somehow fell to savagery, like Rome itself. An ancient stone city may have stood here once, perhaps ruling the lands all around. I firmly believe we shall uncover many marvelous ruins on this site, which shall change the course of our understanding regarding

the lost history of the American continent."

"Big talk for one excavation," I mumbled.

"Hey, I found some articles about the camp being built in 1920," Stacey told me. "That preacher guy and his wife who founded the camp, the Carmodys, moved here from Edenton, North Carolina. He had a church, and his wife Laurie Ann played organ and led the choir. They moved here and created this camp, using some ideas from his Army training. For camp counselors, they hired students from North Georgia Agricultural College over in Dahlonega, which was co-ed."

"Good work," I said.

"Anything happening over there?" Stacey asked.

"Just reading about Tennyford's over-the-top claims that he'd basically found the lost city of Atlantis up on that hill. I can't tell if he was overly imaginative or trying to drum up attention. Maybe he wanted money for future excavations."

I read onward. A total of three articles had been printed about the excavation, the last one listing some of the artifacts Tennyford had found, which I'd already seen in the museum area.

"Further efforts have confirmed my earlier predictions," Tennyford said. "I have always said I believed the Great Stony Owl to be the grave marker of some prominent personage of ancient times, perhaps some pre-Colombian emperor of the Appalachians. Most logically this person was like an Egyptian pharaoh, believed to be a god, worshiped by his people. This headdress of antlers and beads makes as much clear. In addition, he was buried with items of silver and obsidian, which must have been of great value, perhaps sacred and holy."

"This guy made a lot of assumptions," I said. "I wonder if someone a little more fact-based and a little less snake-oily ever studied this site."

A little later, as I was shuffling ahead in search of more articles about Tennyford and Stony Owl, Stacey reached out and grabbed my arm. She was pointing at her glowing screen, mouth working mutely. Then, finally: "Look. July 15, 1929."

I read the front-page headline and felt a chill pass through me.

CAMP COUNSELOR DROWNED AT STONY OWL

A black and white image showed a striking young woman with a big smile, her hair in two thick blond braids under the camp's standard campaign hat.

"Another drowning?" I asked.

"Apparently went out in a canoe alone one night during bad weather and drowned in the lake." Stacey gaped, then gestured toward me as if inviting me to share in her gape. "Just like those boys."

"Except she was alone," I said.

"Or *was* she?" Stacey asked. "What's the real story? Am I right?"

We read over the article. Gwendolyn Malloy of Valdosta, Georgia—several hours south of us, almost to Florida—had been a highly rated student at North Georgia Agricultural College, particularly in the areas of Latin, history, and philosophy. Teachers described a studious and intense girl. The other counselors at the camp, fellow students, described her as serious and hardworking.

If anyone had a motive to kill Gwendolyn, it wasn't apparent in the news article, which was solidly behind the "tragic accident" interpretation of events. She'd been engaged to marry a fellow college student and counselor named Terrance Baker, who was described as grief-stricken. A cop would look at the spouse or significant other first when seeking a murder suspect; my mentor Calvin Eckhart, a former homicide detective turned private paranormal investigator, had taught me that.

Following Gwendolyn's death, the camp had closed for the season. When Stacey looked ahead a year, she didn't find any news of it reopening the following summer. The country had been in throes of the Great Depression by then, so combined with the camp's tragedy of the previous year, it had simply stayed closed, it seemed.

While Stacey was rummaging and sifting her way toward the conclusion that Gwendolyn's drowning had closed down the camp's first incarnation, I was looking through my own old newspapers for word of Tennyford, the bearded amateur archaeologist whose pictures reminded me of that eccentric billionaire who created Jurassic Park.

He showed up again in an October edition of the paper, claiming to have invented a new "apple-growing formula" that had supposedly resulted in a bumper crop at his own orchards. A picture showed Tennyford smiling through his cottony beard, pointing to a brown jug labeled TENNYFORD'S APPLE-GROW.

By early spring, he was dead.

NATURALIST SLAIN BY MOUNTAIN LION

"Yikes," Stacey said, when I pointed it out to her.

"Apparently he came back in early March of 1898 to plan another, larger excavation of the mound," I told her. "Alone. After he'd been missing for several days, a search party formed. They found him in the first place they looked."

"At the owl," Stacey said.

I nodded. "What was left of him. I guess it was back in the *Red Fern* days when they still had mountain lions."

"So, just to be clear," Stacey said, "The guy who came up here, dug into the owl, and pulled out people's bones and burial items later returned here and died horribly."

"Right," I said. "His whole campsite was torn apart."

"I feel like they left some significant details out of the museum display back at the lodge," Stacey said.

"Well, the museum is supposed to help sell the camp to kids and their parents. Not scare people off."

"So the museum is self-serving and biased."

"Exactly. That's two more deaths we've uncovered. Tennyford in 1898 and Gwen in 1929. Thirty years apart."

"You think that's significant?" Stacey asked. "Maybe there's something supernatural that comes back every so often to feed, you think? Like cicadas? Or Pennywise the clown? This thing pops up every thirty years and kills someone? With balloons?"

"I don't know. The years could be a coincidence. But I doubt it's a coincidence that Gwen died the same way as the three boys later would, paddling out in a boat during a storm."

"Hey, sorry, but we did make an overhead announcement." The librarian arrived, a thirtyish lady with purple hair and triangular-rimmed glasses. Purple-flower tattoos ringed her wrist. "We've closed for the evening. We open at nine tomorrow."

"We've been here that many hours?" I looked at my phone. Seven already.

"Yes, and my stomach is eating itself. I can't believe you made me work so long without food." Stacey groaned, hand on her stomach as dramatically as an actress portraying a pregnant character. She rose and cast the librarian a desperate smile. "Where can we eat? Fast is necessary. Good is preferable."

"Everyone loves the Sushi Shack," she said. "They're open until eight."

"Let's run!" Stacey said, grabbing my hand, but I didn't move.

"Do you know whether the historical society is open tomorrow?" I asked the librarian.

"Oh, yeah. My grandma's part of that. It's in the old courthouse in the middle of town, you can't miss it. It's the only place that looks like it time traveled from a fancy part of the nineteenth century. They open at ten." Her eyes wandered to my screen. "What are you... I mean, did y'all find everything you needed?"

"Everything except that sushi." Stacey yanked on my arm, somewhat painfully, her hunger transforming her, werewolf-like, into a complete and total monster.

"We're researching Stony Owl," I said. "Do you know anything about it?"

"I'm sure she just wants to lock up the library and go home," Stacey said irritably.

"Have you heard the Trailwalker legend?" she asked. "They say Stony Owl is guarded by the ghost of the ancient chief who's buried there, and he walks the trails around it at night, stalking anyone who disturbs his grave."

"We have. Do you think there's any truth to it?" I asked, while walking slowly toward the front door. The librarian walked with me. Stacey hurried ahead and waited by the door, glowering impatiently.

"Who can say? There's a reason they call it a legend." She turned off most of the library's lights and led us out the front door, locking it behind her. "I did sneak up there with some friends in high school once. Trying to scare each other. It *was* scary."

"What was scary about it?" I tried to keep my tone casual.

"You just felt like something was up there." Her tone was guarded. "The legend is more fun than the reality, I'll say that much." She'd reached her own car, an old teal Camry. "If you're thinking about going up there, I'd stay away."

"We're actually studying the history of the camp for the new owners," I said.

Now the librarian shook her head. "I hope they know what they're doing."

"Why do you say that?"

"There's been some bad luck there."

"That's what we've been learning," I said. "The boys who drowned there, and Gwendolyn Malloy. And Tennyford before that."

"You really have done your research."

"We're trying to understand what happened in order to make the camp safer for future campers," I said. "But the newspapers haven't told us much. Do you know anybody local who could tell us about the camp? Maybe somebody who worked there, or went there as a camper?"

She seemed to hesitate, then sighed. "I might, but most people aren't too likely to speak to an outsider about it. The legend, sure, but not the real history. Not the darker parts."

"It would help us a lot," I said. "And as a librarian, isn't it your sacred duty to help us find the information we need?"

She looked at me a long moment, then burst into laughter. "Yes, it is. According to the sacred oaths taken by librarians going all the way back to Alexandria."

"That's just what I thought." I gave her one of my cards.

"Private investigator," she read. "How exciting."

"We do get into some weird stuff sometimes," I said. "And we'd really, really appreciate any help you can give us with understanding the history of the camp."

"And I'd really appreciate getting that sushi now." Stacey, the unstoppable hunger-monster, dragged me toward the van.

"It's so good," the librarian said, before climbing into her own car.

Chapter Eighteen

"This is *so* good," Stacey moaned, and she was only on the ginger-dressing salad. I'd moved on to miso soup and pork shumai dumplings. The sushi hadn't even arrived and I already felt confident that we'd found the right place. "That was the world's greatest librarian. She even put the microfilm away for us."

"She probably thought we'd replace it incorrectly, but yeah." I sipped some caffeine-heavy tea, but it was only meant to keep me awake for the drive back to camp. I had no illusions about our ability to stay awake once we saw our beds. "So the camp didn't reopen until 1967. It just sat there, closed, for all those years after Gwen drowned."

"Plus they had the Great Depression and World War Two right after all of that, to really nail down the coffin lid," Stacey said.

"So what did Reverend Carmody and his wife do

next?" I asked. "After the camp closed?"

"I haven't really tracked that down yet," Stacey said. "Why can't libraries be open all night? Like a Waffle House?"

"It's probably not financially feasible—"

"Yeah, yeah, it would just be convenient for us every once in a while. That's what we get for being nocturnal. A world without libraries. Holy cow, look."

The sushi arrived, some savory red tuna for Stacey and that crab I'd been hurting for earlier. Living by the ocean, I may have had doubts about ordering seafood way up in the mountains, but these were utterly obliterated in a matter of seconds.

We ate quickly, since the place was about to close and I wasn't looking forward to a night drive up the steep mountain anyway. Delaying the inevitable would only make it worse. Perhaps I'd be able to see the road by the glowing whites of my knuckles.

Back at camp, we did quick equipment checks where possible before climbing into our bunks at Wolf Cabin. I set my phone alarm for three in the morning, which would give us some hours of contented, belly-filled sleep, but also wake us up for a few hours of deep-night observation time before sunrise.

As it turned out, I wouldn't need my alarm.

The soft voices woke me in the dark depths of the night. I couldn't make out their words. They whispered, then laughed. The voices of kids at play.

I cracked my eyes open, but otherwise remained lying where I was on my bunk. The room was chilly.

They were faint and shadowy, like black cobwebs drifting on a breeze, barely visible as they moved through our room. A shriek of laughter rose—I'd heard that laughter before, over in Bobcat Cabin.

The faint shadow figures slid to the door and vanished.

"Stacey!" I said, but she didn't answer. I hurried to my feet and shook her shoulder. "Stacey!"

Stacey was deep asleep, unresponsive. As I tried to rouse her, the last traces of laughter faded down the hall. The entities were slipping away.

I pulled on my boots, grabbed my flashlight, and followed after them.

They sounded like they'd gone into the common room, but it was quiet and empty when I arrived, so I continued out the front door.

The campground lay silent around me in the dead of night, the fire ring cold and dark. A patch of starry sky looked down through a gap in the tree cover, bringing a little moonlight. No animal sounds, no owls or crickets, just the unsettling silence.

The laughter sounded again, well ahead of me, then stopped abruptly. I continued onward, listening carefully, worried I'd lost the entities.

It sounded again, for just a second, fainter and even more distant. I picked up the pace.

To me, it seemed the entities could have left Bobcat Cabin, crossed through Wolf Cabin where Stacey and I slept, and were now headed up the trail toward...

"The lake," I whispered.

I hesitated, considering going back inside for Stacey, then decided I'd just follow at a distance instead. For all I knew, the apparitions had already vanished.

I hopped off the porch and walked through the cluster of cabins, past the fire ring, toward the trail where I'd last heard the laughter.

The trail was silent too, except for leaves crunching under my boots as I walked alone in the darkness. An owl cackled overheard, startling me.

As I walked the trail, I began to wonder if I'd really been following anything but my imagination. I could hear movement in the woods on either side of the path, likely night creatures on the prowl, but I looked each time to see if they were shadowy children. Since arriving at the camp, I'd heard them, glimpsed them, even dreamed about them, but had never gotten a clear look at them.

Finally, I reached the activity village, with the arts and crafts shack and such, by the lake. Katydids echoed across the water, but I heard no laughter and saw no shadow children.

Then I heard a voice, soft and hesitant: "Hello?"

I froze where I was, in the pavilion that included the picnic tables and the stage end of the arts and crafts hut.

After a bit, the voice spoke again: "Hello?"

It came from the direction of the boathouse and dock. I tiptoed in that direction, heart thumping, wondering what I would find.

"Are you there?" the voice asked. It didn't sound like the laughter or whispers I'd heard. This voice was thicker, fuller, deeper, the voice of a living person.

Edging around the corner of the boathouse, I saw Nate standing out on the end of the dock.

"Hello?" he said again. At first I thought he'd seen me, but I gradually realized he wasn't facing my direction, but instead was looking out at the lake. "I'm here," he said.

He fell quiet and paced back and forth. Clearly he was expecting to meet someone, but I didn't see any sign of a boat paddling across the moonlit water.

Minutes passed. Nate paced for a while, then sat on the end of the dock, his feet dangling over the water. I couldn't help half-expecting some tentacled Cthulhu demon to emerge from the depths and grab his feet, but none did, and he eventually stood and paced again. Occasionally he would call out another "Hello?" Every time something splashed, he'd look over, stepping in that direction, only to be disappointed.

I really had no idea what to make of the situation. I felt bad for spying, but any movement, even walking away, could draw his attention to me. I wondered who he'd been expecting to meet out at the lake so very late. He must have been returning from here when we'd glimpsed him the previous night.

So I watched, quietly as I could, while he paced and waited. The night wasn't going all that well for either of us.

Then something grabbed me from behind and yanked my hair; my ponytail served as a convenient handle for my unexpected assailant. Pain jolted my entire scalp, and I cried out, hurt and surprised all at once.

Oops.

"Hello?" Nate said yet again, but in a very different tone this time. He'd shifted from tentative and hopeful to confused. "Is that you?"

I turned to face my attacker, but I saw nobody.

Laughter shrieked in the air around me for a second, then stopped abruptly.

Something splashed in the lake, near the part of the shore closest to me, but I saw nothing in the moonlight.

Nate's footsteps clomped toward me along the dock, coming my way, as inevitable as a countdown. If I ran now, he'd definitely see me racing across the little village to the path back to the cabins. I wasn't even sure I could outrun the athletic fourteen-year-old. He'd catch up with me, and I'd have no real explanation.

So instead I stood in place and kept facing the water and called out "Is someone there?" just before Nate rounded the corner of the boathouse. He was running, and he had to stop short so he didn't barrel into me.

I shouted and jumped as if surprised, then clicked on my flashlight, pointing it down at his khaki shorts and muddy baseball cleats so I didn't blind him.

"Oh, it's you," he said. "Relax, you're fine."

"Sorry," I told him. "You scared me. I thought I heard voices. Was that you?"

"Did you see anyone else?" He looked past me toward the water.

"I thought I heard someone splashing." I pointed, and he jogged over to the shore and looked down. "What's going on?" I asked.

He hesitated before answering. "Nothing."

"Was someone else here? Or were you expecting someone?"

"I guess not." He turned away from the water. "Were you spying on me or what? Following me around?"

"Spying on you?" I acted offended by the very notion. "How could I have followed you? Were you sneaking around our cabin tonight? Because I thought I heard some voices there, too. Was that you? Wait.. were you spying on us? Peeking in our windows?"

"What? No!" Nate looked a little frightened at my question. He backed up, holding up his hands as if surrendering. "I definitely did not do that. I only came as far as the lake. From my house, back that way." He pointed toward Stony Owl's densely wooded hill.

"So you were planning to meet someone tonight?" I asked.

"No, I..." He sighed. "Don't tell my parents."

"You say that every time I see you. Is something bothering you? If you need someone to talk to—"

"When are you going to be done with your stupid video anyway? It's taking forever."

"We're half-vacationing here," I said. "Free cabin, nice quiet lake to stroll past when you can't sleep. Or when you're meeting someone in secret. What don't you want me to tell you parents? Is it drugs?"

"No! Come on." He looked out at the water. "Just a girl."

"Oh. A secret girl?"

"Yeah." He was looking at the ground, toeing at it with his shoe. The kid was taller than me, about as tall as his older brother, but he suddenly seemed a lot smaller. Was he blushing?

"You meet a girl out here at night?" I asked.

"Don't *tell* anyone."

"Okay, but what's the big secret?"

"I have a girlfriend back home."

"Back in Atlanta?"

"Johns Creek, technically. It's a separate city. But, uh, yeah. But that's like two hours away. All we can do is text."

"Okay." I was now officially uncomfortable with this conversation and ready to disappear as soon as possible. "Well, it's none of my business, but you should probably be honest with everybody involved. Who's the girl you're seeing here?"

"I'm going home." Nate turned and started along the trail that would wind past the hill toward his family's house.

"I really don't mind talking." I fell into step beside him.

"Good luck with your video." He put on speed, not quite running, but rapidly putting distance between us. "Bye."

I stopped, letting him hustle off into the shadows. The only alternative was to stalk him all the way home, demanding more information he clearly didn't want to give. Not the best way to treat a client's kid, especially when there was a good argument that this was indeed none of my business.

"Remember, the lake's dangerous!" I called after him. "Four people have drowned out there."

He didn't look back.

Returning to the lake shore, I looked out over the water, listening carefully. I heard a few splashes, but no more voices.

I swept the surface of the water with my flashlight beam, and even had a look under the dock, but nobody was there.

The trail had an eerie feeling as I walked back to the cabin. I kept checking over my shoulder, thinking someone might be following me, maybe whatever jerk of an entity had pulled my hair. I officially hated the invisible giggler now.

I saw nothing, but I kept my light on until I was back inside.

Chapter Nineteen

"Where did you go?" Stacey asked, meeting me as I entered the common room. "I was super-nonplussed to wake up alone in this cabin at four in the morning. I thought the ghosts had carried you off. Or you'd gone to the bathhouse without your flip-flops. I wasn't sure which was worse."

"I heard some voices and followed them."

"Without waking me?"

"I tried. You were resistant and sullen."

"Well, glad you're in one piece. And that you didn't take a barefoot shower at camp. Where did the voices lead you?"

"Over by the lake." I caught her up on the situation.

"Ooh, so Nathan's got a local girlfriend. Not that surprising. And he's keeping her secret from his other girlfriend. What a little charmer he's turning out to be. Like a snake charmer. Or more like a charming snake, picking up girls in every town and breaking their hearts—"

"Anyway, that's why he's sneaking out at night. That's a problem for us, since he's not supposed to know we're paranormal investigators searching for ghosts at night."

"Hopefully someone tells him, maybe the brother, so we don't have to dance around that little snake too long."

"But for now, keep the little snake charmed." I shook my head. "I told him not to go down to the lake alone."

"Good idea. What do you think about this girl he's seeing? Could she be, you know, a ghost?"

"If she was, she's got him fooled. That would take a powerful apparition. You try to get information out of him, he likes you better." I headed into the second bunk room to view the Bobcat Cabin monitors. Stacey followed me and watched as I accessed the night's recordings.

"Just checking for activity around the time they woke me up," I said.

The night vision camera had nothing for us. The thermal was more interesting, catching that broad, dispersed cold spot rolling through like a fog.

The audio had the most to offer.

It came in patches, like some annoying kid had grabbed a remote and kept turning the volume up and down at random. Laughter. A yell. A few running footsteps. A squeak and a scrape like one of the bunk beds being pushed aside, though nothing visibly moved inside the room. It was just like when I'd pursued the invisible giggler in that same cabin, the auditory apparitions starting and stopping abruptly, lasting only briefly.

"Wow," Stacey said. "Sounds like the night campers came back."

"And passed through here on their way to the lake. I

wonder why they were going there."

"If it's those three boys, or Gwendolyn, they'd be revisiting the scene of their death."

"If it's them." I nodded. "We should check whether Bobcat Cabin was the home of the boys who drowned. That would fit the picture."

"Maybe you could ask Josh."

"We're on cracking ice with Josh as it is. He was angry at the idea that those kids he knew could be haunting the place." I stood up and drew on my jacket. "Come on, let's hike up to the lodge. There's something I want to check out."

At the lodge parking lot, we checked the van, verifying that our equipment was still up and recording.

Inside the lodge, the ghosts of burning logs past filled my nostrils, as usual, as if trying to make me nostalgic for other people's lost childhoods. We passed through the utility closet, stepped over a fallen broom and through the folding doors, up through the narrow stairway to the attic. We made our way past the old sports equipment to the metal filing cabinets shoved against one side of the mock cabin, not far from the dusty fireplace.

"Yay, more paperwork," Stacey said as I pulled open a drawer.

"We need to go around Josh to get a more detailed picture of the past," I said. "So we're collecting contact information for everyone who was here that final year when the three boys died. Campers, counselors, anyone. Emphasis on people with nearby addresses."

"But that contact information is thirty years old, and it would mostly be the parents of people who lived here."

"On top of that, this is before the era of universal

email and cell phone numbers that follow you. So, yep,
probably a lot of hay, not a lot of needles." I handed Stacey
a stack of file folders. "You start with campers A through
E. Make a checklist of everyone we need to call."

She sighed. "Fine. I guess I'll spread them out on that
old ping-pong table. Once I clear off the slide projector
and what I assume will be some disgusting colonies of bugs
and spiders."

"That's the spirit," I said, taking F through M for
myself. I set them atop the file cabinets and started flipping
through papers and harvesting data, twentieth-century style.
So basically just copying things into my notebook.

It was much too early to cold call people at home; the
sun wasn't even up yet. By the time it got to be a decent
hour, though, Josh might be poking around, and he might
not approve of us calling old campers from his childhood,
especially not to talk about the boys' deaths. Hopefully
Allison wouldn't let him fire us before we found some
answers.

I wrote a checklist of campers and contact info, but
paused when I opened one of the files. I flipped back in
my notepad to confirm the name.

Thomas Fortenberry.

I was looking at the file of one of the dead campers.

I read it over. Thomas had attended Camp Stony Owl
for four years, starting when he was eleven. He'd been
fourteen when he'd died in the lake. There was contact
information for his family down in Macon, but I had zero
intention of ever calling his family to ask about their dead
son. The file noted that he preferred active sports, was
restless when it came to quieter activities.

After a minute, I closed the file and slid it into my

backpack for later, then resumed gathering contact information about other campers.

We put everything back before sunrise and hurried downstairs. If Josh didn't find out we were combing through the files, he couldn't tell us to stop doing it.

After sunrise, we drove into town and stopped for breakfast at the Skillet Cafe, which served plenty of country-fried mountain-climbing fare: platters of pancakes and sausage, grits and eggs, gravy and biscuits, things Stacey was in the mood for and devoured. I ordered a bagel and picked at it. I was nervous about trying to reach out to witnesses.

My phone chimed, and I glanced at the text message. "Who is it?"

"The librarian might have a lead. I'll head outside and call her back. You pay for breakfast."

"Oh, yeah, convenient division of labor," Stacey said as I left.

Outside, I took a moment to breathe in the warming mountain air. The town was tiny and picturesque, nestled in mountainous wilderness on all sides. I looked down the road toward the library as I called her back, not that I could see the little building from here. It was close, though.

"Hi," she said. "It's Winnie, the librarian from yesterday?"

"Thanks for getting back to me," I said.

"So, I thought about what you said. My great-grandmother actually went to Camp Stony Owl a long time ago. She was there when the counselor girl drowned."

"Wow. Do you think she'd talk to us about it?"

"That's the thing. This is a small town, and there are certain things people won't want to discuss with outsiders.

Meemaw will be happy to tell you about the more cheerful side of local history—she used to volunteer at the county historical society, over in the old courthouse, until she was almost ninety. But this is something dark and tragic. I've tried to explain that you need to hear about the dangers, about what happened to the kids. Anyway, she's agreed to meet you, at least, but I don't make any promises."

"That's great!"

"Have I kept to my sacred librarian oaths now?" she asked.

"Definitely. Thank you so much."

When Stacey emerged from the restaurant, I filled her in.

We drove to an assisted living home just outside town. Along the way, we crossed a bright blue lake. A couple of sailboats were out gliding in the spring sunshine. It looked much more appealing than paddling the black lake water at Stony Owl.

At the nursing home, Winnie came out to meet us and led us to a sunny room with a high ceiling and a fireplace, though the day was too warm for a fire.

"This is my great-grandmother, Mrs. Winifred Barrister," the librarian said. "I was named after her."

Mrs. Barrister occupied a wheelchair, parked in front of a card table by the window. She was a slight, birdlike woman, fragile-looking but with bright eyes. Though she was in her nursing home recreation room, she was dressed in a pantsuit and pearls, as if going to an office later.

"You'll have to excuse me," she told the frowning, heavily mustached man across from her. A game of chess occupied the table between them.

"You don't have to apologize for beating me. I can see

how this will turn out." He stood, put on a hat. "One day, I will checkmate you."

"You're learning, anyway," she replied, smiling.

The man nodded at us as he stepped out of the room, heading for an outdoor garden area.

"Who was that, Meemaw?" Winnie asked as we took nearby chairs.

"He's a feisty young thing," Mrs. Barrister said. "Just eighty-three. If only he'd shave that mustache. And he's not very good at chess."

"When Meemaw turned a hundred, she got letters from the president, from the governor, from everyone," Winnie said. "Isn't that right, Meemaw?"

"Not Johnny Carson, though," Mrs. Barrister said. "I always did like him."

"Meemaw, this is Ellie and Stacey. They're in town doing some historical research—"

"Have they been to the old courthouse?" Mrs. Barrister interrupted.

"Not yet, ma'am," I said. "We passed it earlier—"

"You must go. I'd give you a tour myself, but I had to stop when I hit my nineties. Doctor insisted. My daughter will show you around when you go. It's a fine museum." Mrs. Barrister went on to speak in great detail about the town's historic courthouse and the displays inside, which apparently included antique tools and a room full of miniatures and dollhouses.

I nodded along, not wanting to interrupt and seem rude, but watching for any opening to steer the conversation to the camp.

"They're actually researching Stony Owl, Meemaw," Winnie cut in, after a few minutes. "Like I was explaining earlier."

"Are they?" Mrs. Barrister adjusted her glasses as if to study us. "It's been closed a long time."

"Our clients are reopening it this summer," I said.

"That's not wise." She shook her head.

"Why not?"

"There's been a lot of bad luck up there."

"We've learned all about the boys, Paul and Thomas and Kyle. Our client knew them; they attended Camp Stony Owl together. What we don't know much about is the counselor who drowned, Gwendolyn Malloy. It seems like her death was very similar to the boys' deaths. The more we can learn, the more we can make the campground safe."

Mrs. Barrister looked at us for a long moment, as if judging us carefully, then sighed.

"I suppose I could discuss it a little, if it's for the safety of the children. Do not take this as me condoning the return of that campground, however."

"I understand, ma'am." I gripped my pen tight, eager to take notes.

"Gwendolyn Malloy." Mrs. Barrister's gaze drifted out the window, to the fuzzy pink mimosa tree outside. "She was a beauty. She was my counselor those last two years."

"What year did you attend Camp Stony Owl?" I asked.

"I went in '26, '27, and '28. That first year, I was like a frightened little knock-kneed girl who didn't dare speak to anyone...by the end of that first summer, I never wanted to leave. Not the camp, not my fellow Rabbits from Rabbit Cabin. Those girls were like sisters to me." Her eyes had a faraway look behind her glasses. She was starting to open up to us, as if this were a topic that some part of her really wanted to discuss, even if it was with oddball outsiders like us. "And part of me never did. I still dream about the good times. There was some magic there, I believe. Not necessarily bad magic. For me, it gave me strength. But maybe it's what you make of it. And what got made of it was so tragic in the end."

"When did you meet Gwendolyn Malloy?" I asked.

"When she was my counselor, my second year. She was as pretty as a princess. Mean as one, too. I was Rabbit Cabin all three years. We were the best cabin on the girls' side, but then I'm partial."

"So Gwendolyn wasn't the friendliest counselor?" I asked.

"Not if you were beneath her. She could put on the charm when she wanted, though. Such as when the boy counselors were around, or the boss."

"Reverend Carmody?" I asked.

"He was such a stern man. Stern and distant. To a young girl like me, he was a bit like God himself. Thank you, dear," she told Winnie, who placed a freshly brewed mug of tea in front of her.

"What about his wife, Laurie Ann?"

She smiled. "Mrs. Laurie Ann was sweet as sugar pie, or properly made tea. She always had a hug and a kiss for everyone. She was the sweetest. She seemed a mismatch for the Reverend. He was ex-Army, you know. Big, strong, angry-looking man. We were all glad Mrs. Laurie Ann was there to take his rough edges off."

"I heard Gwendolyn died at the camp," I said. "Is that accurate?"

"Oh, yes, that was the end of everything. It was tragic. Miss Gwen let her feelings run away with her."

"Her feelings about what?"

Mrs. Barrister looked uncomfortable. "Maybe you should go," she told Winnie. "This isn't appropriate talk for children."

"I'm thirty-two, Meemaw."

"Already? Time does run downhill, doesn't it? Steeper each year." She shook her head. "What were we discussing?"

"How Gwendolyn let her feelings run away with her."

"Oh, yes. She was engaged to another counselor, Mister Terrance. They went to the same college, too. The first summer they worked at the camp, you could see they were courting each other, but she played hard to get. She could play that because so many boys liked her. Mister Terrance was the prize catch, though. By the following summer, they were engaged to be married, and Gwendolyn loved to show off the pricey ring he'd bought her. Even if she'd showed it to you and told you all about it before, she'd do it again, whether you asked for a repeat performance or not.

"Well, she would sneak Mister Terrance into her room at night, against the Reverend's strict fraternization rules. One or two of us would always go spy on them. They were only kissing," she added a little sharply, glancing at her great-granddaughter, who nodded. "But it was scandalous. And fascinating, if you want the truth. Like a romance novel. Maybe we didn't warm to Miss Gwendolyn like a friend, but I suppose we all wanted to be *like* her a little bit. And we wanted her to like us. The colder she was, the more we tried to win her favor.

"Well, Terrance was a handsome boy, and charming— Gwendolyn would pick the finest apple in the barrel, and they said his family had oodles of money, too. But when he slipped in at night, Gwen always reminded him they were not married yet. I'm sure you understand. I doubt boys have changed much." She cast another concerned look at her thirty-two-year-old descendant as though worried about corrupting her.

I smiled but said little, jotting notes, absorbing every word.

"So Terrance got right upset as the summer went on," she continued. "And he found he could get more of what he wanted elsewhere."

"He started dating someone else?"

"Right there under Gwendolyn's nose. He didn't even have the decency to end the engagement first." Mrs. Barrister shook her head.

"Was it another counselor?" I asked.

"No, ma'am." Mrs. Barrister sipped her tea. Almost like she enjoyed dragging this out. Her eyes twinkled. "Winnie, I can't speak about this in front of you."

"Meemaw, I'm—"

"I know how old you are. Would you mind stepping out into the garden? You can look at one of those pocket phones you all love to stare at these days."

"Oh, actually I do need to check my messages." Winnie hurried away, drawing out her phone. Mrs. Barrister smiled wryly after her, the way she'd smiled after beating her gentleman friend at chess.

"These kids today." Mrs. Barrister looked at me and Stacey and gave a *hmph*, as if noticing we were even younger than her great-granddaughter. Just a couple of kids out on a jaunt in our jalopy, that was Stacey and me.

"So you were talking about Terrance's affair?" I said, my pencil touching my notepad again. "It wasn't with another counselor?"

"No."

"Ew, it wasn't a camper though, right?" Stacey winced.

"Terrance got involved with Mrs. Laurie Ann." Mrs. Barrister said this very softly, like a jeweler placing a delicate crystal on silk, presenting the piece of information like a rare treasure she knew we'd appreciate.

Appreciate we did—Stacey and I both dropped our jaws at that, at which the elderly lady smiled. Conversational checkmate, I suppose. Or at least a shocking piece of news.

"The counselor guy had an affair with the preacher's wife?" Stacey asked, in a whisper loud enough to turn more than one silver head in the room away from their books and card games.

Mrs. Barrister nodded slowly, appreciating our appreciation of the great importance of this.

"How did you hear about this?" I asked, by way of gently checking her sources.

"A couple of us Rabbits eavesdropped on Miss Gwendolyn telling another girl counselor about it. Miss Gwen was in tears. She'd gone to Terrance's cabin to surprise him by sneaking in the window, but Mrs. Laurie Ann was already in his room with him. So Gwen came back and cried, and the other girl tried to comfort her. Said she'd never felt so betrayed."

"What happened next?" I asked. It was pretty much all I could say.

"Miss Gwendolyn went out late the next night. We all pretended to be asleep when she checked out. Some of us watched her out the window as she walked away. I'll never forget it, because a storm was coming, and we could see her plain as day each time the lightning flashed. That was the last we saw of her. I wasn't there when they pulled her out of the lake, thank heavens. But after that, we were all sent home. The magic of those summers ended in such horrible tragedy."

"Did the police investigate her death?" I asked.

"Oh, yes. Well, first there was the search party. She went missing for a couple of days, you see. The police led the search. It took some time to find her body because it was in the deep part of the lake, what we called the Cold Hole, because it was so deep the water felt icy even in summer. You had to hold your breath and swim far down, and it gets dark down there." She shivered. "We'd swim as deep as we could, or as deep as we dared. I never cared for that part of the lake, truly. I liked where it was sunny and warm, and I could get to the shallows quick if need be.

"There's one thing the newspapers didn't say, out of respect for the family. And I only say it now because there's hardly anybody left alive to remember. In those days, everybody at Camp Stony Owl wore uniforms. Girls, whether campers or counselors, wore long skirts, and the skirts had pockets."

"Nice," Stacey said.

"When they found Miss Gwendolyn, well." She shook her head. "Her pockets were filled with rocks. A canoe was caught in the brambles on the far shore from the camp, and later they found a broken oar. She'd paddled out in the middle of a storm to drown herself, you see. Thrown herself into the Cold Hole, the deepest part of the lake. Everyone knew where to find it."

"That's so sad," Stacey said. "Just because her boyfriend cheated on her. The snake."

"So it's believed that she committed suicide?" I asked.

"Officially, it was an accident. Out of respect. But we all knew, once we heard about those rocks. That girl drowned herself."

"Whatever happened to the male counselor?" I asked.

"Terrance? Who knows? I guess he left when everyone else did. The camp closed down because of Gwendolyn's death, you see. So everyone scattered back to their hometowns."

"Do you know where they were from? Gwendolyn or Terrance?"

"I'm sorry, no. If I knew, I certainly don't remember now."

"What about Reverend and Mrs. Carmody? What became of them after the camp closed?'

"Reverend Carmody died that winter. He was still living at the campground, you see. I suppose he had nowhere else to go."

"He died the winter after Gwendolyn?"

"Yes."

"How did he die?"

"I believe they said he slipped and fell in the bathtub. Broke his skull. So he died alone there." Her voice dropped to a low, conspiratorial whisper. "They think he probably slipped in November, but they didn't find him until December. It's lucky it was so cold. Half the water in his tub was frozen. Preserved him pretty good for the funeral."

Stacey and I were silent for a moment, letting that sink in.

"What about his wife, Laurie Ann?" I finally asked. "Where was she?"

"She was already gone by then."

"Also deceased?

"Oh, no. After the camp went bust, Laurie Ann up and left."

"She divorced him?"

"Back then, around here, folks didn't get divorced. They had a notion if you swore something in a church before the Lord, that it meant something. It meant there'd be hell to pay if you broke that vow. Pardon my Hollywood language, but it's true. So folks didn't get divorced. But sometimes, if things got bad enough, they up and left. And that's just what Mrs. Laurie Ann did to Reverend Carmody. She up and left."

"Do you know where she might have gone after that?"

"I wouldn't have the foggiest idea, darling."

"And Terrance, the boyfriend?"

"I don't know. I'm sorry. I wasn't close to any of these people, you understand. I don't know where they went after camp closed."

"I understand. Thank you. You've really helped us."

"It's unfortunate to reopen the campground now," she said. "I still say it's better off in the hands of the wild beasts."

After that, she quickly returned the conversation to the subject of the courthouse-turned-museum where she'd volunteered with the historical society, a topic that cheered her a bit after the gloomy talk of death and drowning.

Stacey and I thanked her profusely before leaving.

"Well, that told us a lot," Stacey said.

"But maybe raised more questions than answers." I flipped through my little pocket notepad. I'd started a fresh one for this case, and it was half-full already. "We ought to find out whatever happened to the boyfriend, Terrance, and the preacher's wife, Laurie Ann, to start with."

"It sounds like everyone dies right there. The amateur archaeologist, Tennyford, ripped up by a mountain lion. Then this girl Gwendolyn drowns with her pockets full of rocks, an apparent suicide. But maybe that's just what they *want* us to think. Well, not us specifically, because we hadn't been born at the time, but you know what I mean."

"Right. If Gwendolyn was murdered, stuffing her pockets with rocks would be a way to try to cover it up. Whether she killed herself or was murdered, that kind of emotional trauma can lead right to a haunting."

"But we haven't seen a mysterious girl around the lake."

"Nathan has," I said, and Stacey's eyes widened as I started the van.

Chapter Twenty

Our research continued with a stop by the *North Georgia News*'s office and printing facility, but unfortunately they had little else to offer us about Stony Owl's history. The reporter who'd covered the three boys' deaths had unfortunately passed in the intervening decades. The current staff couldn't offer much beyond articles we'd already seen and the chipper press release Allison and Josh had sent to announce the camp's reopening.

At the courthouse, we were able to verify that the deaths of Gwendolyn Malloy and Reverend Roger Carmody had occurred at the camp and were listed as accidents. No local records existed for Laurie Ann Carmody; she'd skipped town and never returned, as far as we could tell.

Before we left town for the spotty cell reception of the campground, I sat in the van, still parked outside the courthouse, and called my old friend Grant Patterson of the Savannah Historical Association back home. A semi-retired lawyer and full-time gossip, Grant could be a great resource for hard to find information.

"Ellie! Fantastic to hear from you," he said. "It's been too long."

"It really has."

"I hope you're calling with a haunting adventure in which I might share. It's been a rather dull week. My most exciting moment was picking the spring plantings for the Tour of Gardens. I don't know why I let them keep the old family home in the event. It's dreadfully troubling opening one's home to the public. Which is why I'll be staying at Jack Taylor's house on Tybee for the duration."

"It sounds stressful."

"I only wish it were more so. I am so desperately in need of a challenge that I could almost go into the office and attend to my legal practice. Now, please, draw me into your latest bout of supernatural mischief."

I gave him a very quick overview, avoiding personal information about our clients and focusing on the history of Stony Owl.

"Ah, yes, one of the forgotten birds, along with Rock Hawk," he said. "I've read so little about them. There was the hypothesis that Rock Eagle and Rock Hawk were not eagles at all, but buzzards, a sort of bird that might carry the soul to the afterlife. Perhaps it represented an ancient god or spirit."

"There doesn't seem to be much known about any of them," I said.

"I will endeavor to find all I can, but I make no promises."

"Thank you. I was also wondering whether you might know anyone at the University of North Georgia."

"Oh, yes. There's Frances Bering, I believe she chairs the languages department now—"

"We need some information on a student."

"That could be tricky, due to privacy policies—"

"From a hundred years ago, when it was an agricultural school."

Grant chuckled. "It was never an agricultural school, regardless of its name. It was, in fact, a grand little academy, a jewel in the mountains, the first coeducational college in the state. Literature, philosophy, history, science, Greek, and Latin, yes. Agriculture? No, not particularly."

"The student was there in the late 1920s. Terrance Baker. We'd like to know his hometown and anything else you might dig up on him. He worked at Camp Stony Owl during the summer."

"I'll see what I can do."

"We'd also be interested in whatever can be learned about another student who worked there at the same time. Gwendolyn Malloy."

"And these former counselors haunt the camp to this very day?" Grant asked, in the sort of voice one might use when telling a campfire ghost story.

"It's possible. We're still trying to identify the entities. And if you feel like getting some extra credit, we're also trying to trace the fate of one Laurie Ann Carmody, who founded Camp Stony Owl along with her husband Roger. They previously lived in Edenton, North Carolina. We don't know what happened to her after 1929. She may not have gone by the name Carmody after that, either, because she up and left her husband."

"Up and left, I see. Do you have a maiden name? A town of birth?"

"Not so far, unless it's Edenton."

"I shall see what I can find. I look forward to the sleuthing. Is there anything else?"

"That seems like plenty," I said. "Thanks so much."

"The pleasure is overwhelmingly mine," he replied.

After that, Stacey and I visited a local place called Cabin Coffee and took an outdoor table. Armed with hot beverages, we started cold calling our list of campers from the year the three boys had died. I wasn't surprised we didn't get many answers since we were unknown callers. Many numbers had been disconnected, and we scratched them off. Others went to voice mail, but with names that didn't match the family names from the files. We left messages all the same.

Then we drove back up to the campground, under the heavy shadows of the trees, hoping for a nibble on some of the many lines we'd dropped into the water.

Chapter Twenty-One

Back in our cabin, Stacey checked through some of the ocean of data we'd collected from around the campground, looking for moments when motion detectors had been activated or audio recordings had spiked.

I worked on pulling my notes together in a more coherent way, creating a timeline of known events through the campground's history.

We knew of six deaths on site. I listed them in order:

Charles Tennyford – local farmer who excavated the owl, found mauled next to owl, apparent animal attack

Gwendolyn Malloy – counselor who drowned with rocks in her pockets

Rev. Roger Carmody – created the first version of the

camp, died in the bathtub

Paul, Thomas, Kyle – the boys who'd died after going out on a boat in a storm

"Water," I murmured. It was the common element among all the deaths, except for Tennyford.

"What's that?" Stacey asked, crunching on some puffed-rice snack that did not interest me. "You thirsty?"

"I think Josh knows more about why those boys went out on the water that night."

"Yeah, that was pretty obvious."

"But why didn't he want to tell us?" I rubbed my temples. "I hate when the clients don't cooperate. It's like trying to fight with a hand tied behind your back."

"Against an invisible opponent," Stacey added. "Most of the time."

Later, as we hiked up to the lodge, our phones pinged out notification chimes as we entered signal range. I had a few voice mails.

"I think these are people I called earlier," Stacey said, looking at her screen. "Former campers."

"Start calling them back." We entered the lodge and continued through the utility closet and up the stairs.

While Stacey sat down at the ping-pong table, I rifled through the file cabinets, going back in time as fast as I could, back to the beginning of the campground.

The oldest paperwork was packed into a thick, crumbling paper envelope in a bottom drawer. I opened it as carefully as I could manage, but the envelope was so old it fell apart in my hands.

Inside, I found fragile yellow records of Carmody's

purchase of the land from a local bank. A hand-drawn plat showed the hundreds of acres he'd bought. The stone owl effigy did not appear to be any kind of officially designated landmark, then or now.

More paperwork detailed the sale of the preacher's old home in Edenton, North Carolina. Then, under that—

"Jackpot!" I shouted at Stacey, wincing as I realized she was on the phone. I'd been screening out her phone conversations with former campers while I cabinet dived. She glanced at me, and I waved it off and shook my head.

"I'm sorry, sir," Stacey said, turning back toward the cleared spot on the ping-pong table. "Could you repeat that last part again?"

I'd been searching for Laurie Ann's maiden name. If she'd up and left her husband, she might have reverted back to it.

I'd found their marriage certificate from Edenton, North Carolina. Roger Carmody had married Laurie Ann Wilkerson in 1915. I had her surname and her place of birth, which was indeed Edenton. What I needed was a place of death, though. And she could have ended up anywhere.

I copied the information off the marriage certificate and replaced the papers as carefully as I could. Stacey wrapped up her phone call.

"Well, that was detailed," she said. "That guy kept going on and on about his memories of the camp. He was kind of reluctant to talk about the three drowned boys and the camp closure. He said he didn't really know them, because he was Warthog Cabin and a little younger. He went on and on about how it was their own fault for going out on the water in the storm. He remembers being sad that the place never reopened."

"Wow. Good memories despite the trauma. And I found the full name of the preacher's wife: Laurie Ann Wilkerson."

A floorboard creaked, very distinctly, as if in response to the sound of that name.

We looked at the cabin structure in the back corner of the attic. Did something shift behind the window? The interior was completely dark beyond the glass.

I started toward the cabin's door, thinking again how odd it seemed to build a cabin inside the attic. Maybe it had been nice and cozy in its day. It certainly didn't look that way now.

With Stacey at my back, I turned the knob and eased open the cabin door. Its creaky, scraping hinges were entirely non-soothing.

The interior of the cabin was as we'd seen it before, dim and cluttered, jumbled and disorganized, bedroom furniture buried under boxes and paint cans and junk.

"It's cold," Stacey whispered, and I nodded, shivering.

As we stood there adjusting to the deeper gloom, I became aware of a shadow in the bathroom doorway. It was so completely, perfectly still that I wondered if my eyes were playing tricks on me, drawing human forms where there were none, as our eyes can do in dim places, turning a coat on a hanger into Slenderman staring at us from the closet.

Even when my eyes adjusted to the gloom, the shadow remained, darker than the space around it, untouched by the feeble yellow lamp light from our work space in the main attic area behind us.

I nudged Stacey. She nodded; she saw it, too. I was glad

I'd gone with the buddy system on this one. To heck with the Rule of One.

The shadow was featureless, but I could discern the outline of a wide brim, exactly like the campaign hat the Reverend had worn. The preacher had died right there, in the small bathroom where the shadow stood.

"Reverend Carmody?" I asked. My fingers rested on my flashlight, but I didn't dare draw it and shed light. "Roger Carmody? Is that you?"

It didn't respond. The shadow was as unmoving as a mannequin.

I stepped closer. Stacey followed a few paces behind, recording with a handheld camera, doing her part while I did mine.

"I'm here to help," I said in a soft voice, trying not to run him off. Carmody had died suddenly in his tub, decades earlier, and was possibly failing to process this reality. "I can help you move on. I've helped many do that." *And captured others and stuck them deep in the ground.* I kept that thought to myself.

The floorboard squeaked again and the shadow slipped out of sight, deeper into the bathroom.

"Don't go disappearing on me again, Reverend." I took a breath and stepped through the door. Stacey hung back, filming from the doorway, since there was barely enough room for one person to turn around.

The room was cold, but the shadow figure was gone.

"Reverend Carmody?" I looked around at the little sink with its rust-splotched pipe, the medicine cabinet open, his old straight razor on the steel shelf within.

A metallic rattling sound made me jump, and I held up my hands, thinking the razor was being flung at me by an invisible entity.

The sound had come from behind me, though.

I turned to see the handles and faucets in the tub rattling as though someone had kicked them. Dark water gushed from the faucet, splattering the dusty old tub and soaking the cardboard boxes stored there.

Stacey gasped. I turned in time to see the door slam shut, sealing her outside the bathroom and trapping me inside.

I stood in pitch darkness, cut off from Stacey. She banged on the door, yelling, but couldn't force it open.

The room grew colder. I drew my flashlight, and it took all my willpower to leave it off, to resist the urge to drive the entity away.

"Carmody," I said, trying to sound commanding. "I'm listening. Speak to me."

A smell like sour fish, like wet and rotten decay, filled the tiny room. The stench flooded my nostrils and lungs, gagging me.

The entity was back; I couldn't see it, but I could certainly feel it, a solid, cold, reeking mass occupying the space in front of me, blocking my path to the door.

"Carmody. Are you stuck here? Are you trapped in the place—"

A cold hand struck me in the chest, right in the sternum. I toppled back into the tub, landing on the cardboard boxes stored there. They slipped aside with a sloshing sound.

I dropped deeper, sitting in frigid, sour-smelling water that smelled like a lake instead of a bath.

"Enough!" I shouted, firing up my light.

The white glow revealed the figure leaning over me.

The apparition was more solid now, more than a shadow, dressed in a pale uniform like the one in the pictures downstairs.

The campaign hat shadowed most of its face, but this was probably for the best. The skin I could see was pale, bloated, and loose, badly decayed.

The cold, dark water rose higher around me.

"Don't you dare try to drown—" I began, but yeah, that's what happened next.

Clammy fingers closed around my mouth; the wet skin was squishing, sliding around on the tips of its finger bones. The decayed fingers felt slender like bones, but sharp and strong.

The entity shoved me under the surface, overflowing the tub and sloshing water over the side as I went under.

I finally managed to activate the speaker on my belt, filling the room with The Old Kentucky Boys Bluegrass Gospel, belting out "Revive Us Again." I could distantly hear the banjo and fiddle accompaniment through the thick, sour water filling my ears. And my nose. Ugh.

The dead thing's grip loosened. I kicked out and shoved my way up. The ghost wasn't solid enough for me to hit back—a huge advantage on the ghost's part—but the music seemed to have some effect. Maybe the holy music would help the dead reverend recall his life a bit, distract him with memories, even speak to his better nature, if he had one.

I regained my feet and pushed loose, wet hair from my face. I doubted I'd ever get the stink out of my shirt, or my skin.

My flashlight filled the room with searing white light. The apparition was gone.

The door flew open and Stacey staggered in. I caught her before she could slip on the flooded floor and take her own sour lake-water bath.

"Oh." She hugged me close, perhaps completely misunderstanding my intention. "Are you okay?"

"Yeah. Fine. Sorry about the smell." I backed off of her.

"Huh? I guess it is kinda musty." She shone her light around. "The shadow guy gave you the old slipperoo again, huh?"

"He tried to drown me." I pointed to the tub.

It held a couple of cardboard boxes, partly crushed from my close encounter with them, and lots of dust.

Looking down, I found dust all over my jacket. I could taste it on my tongue, where only moments before there had been rank water.

"I'm completely dry," I said.

"Okay. Uh, guess the new antiperspirant's working?" Stacey drew back from me.

"No, I was just drowning..." I stared at the tub. It looked like no water had touched it in years. "They wore one of the old camp uniforms. Maybe it was Reverend Carmody. It looked like a drowning victim."

"Could be one of the boys, then. No, wait. The uniforms were phased out. What about the counselor guy Terrance? Gwendolyn's boyfriend?"

"Possibly, or Gwendolyn herself, or Carmody's wife, Laurie Ann, or any soul from that era still attached to this place might appear in the camp uniform. But Reverend Carmody is the one who died right here."

We looked at the bath tub again, then hurried downstairs and out the back door. It was definitely time to get out of the lodge.

Chapter Twenty-Two

Outside, we hurried away from the shadow of the lodge, out to the large fire ring behind it.

"We'd better stop here." I sat on one of the tree-trunk benches at the fire pit, and Stacey took another. We couldn't travel too far from the lodge and its satellite dish until we'd returned some calls.

We both faced the lodge. Neither of us wanted to turn our backs on its dark windows.

My first callback was a guy named Trevor Knowles of Baldwin, Georgia, who'd been at the camp in its final year. He was two years younger than Josh. I knew nothing about him other than some details in his folder. He liked arts and crafts and had won a yellow ribbon on the ropes course.

"My mom told me you'd called asking about the old camp," he said, once we'd started talking. "It's funny, I've been having a lot of dreams about it here lately. Getting back into painting, like when I was a kid. Painting and whittling."

"What kind of dreams?"

"Just memories, mostly. Being a kid, running around, splashing in the lake. Those were good times. I only went there two summers, but I remember it a lot. Kids these days don't have summer camps like that, probably. Something special about that place."

"Did you know the three boys who drowned?"

"Well, they were Bobcats," he said. "I was a Wolf. I was twelve, which put me in the younger room at Wolf Cabin. The Bobcats that died were fourteen or fifteen. That was a big age difference to us back then, you might remember from your own teenage years. So I saw them around, but didn't have a lot of activities with them."

"What do you remember about them?"

"The four of them pretty much acted like they ruled the place. Older guys, like I said."

"I thought there were three?"

"Three that died, but four in their gang."

"Who was the fourth?"

"Uh..." He blew a raspberry sound. "Give me a minute."

"We have Thomas, Paul, and Kyle."

"Oh, yes. And the fourth one was called John. Joe? Jim... no. Josh. Josh, that's it."

"Josh."

"Pretty sure. Jeb? No, back up one. Josh."

"Josh Conner?"

"Maybe. But he didn't die with the others, anyway."

"Do you know if he was with them that night?" I asked.

"It would be strange if he wasn't. They were a pack."

"Can you think of any reason Josh wouldn't have gone out in the boat with the others?"

"Like I said, I didn't know those older Bobcats that well. I guess Josh was just smarter than the others. There was a storm that night, you know. And it's kind of like that thing your momma probably asked you growing up—if all your friends jumped off a cliff, would you? And he was the one who wouldn't. The one who didn't jump, that's Josh."

"Did you see Josh afterward? Speak to him, maybe?"

"Not after the storm and the boys went missing. Camp closed down and never opened again. I wasn't happy about it. It's like when you wake up from a good dream into a bad morning. Or walk out of a good movie and back into a bad reality. I guess I understand it now, though. Nobody wants to send their kids to some camp where kids died. Only dumb characters in horror movies do that. And people who hate their kids, maybe. Could be a market for it, come to think."

"Have you heard the camp is reopening?"

"Is it really now?" He sounded almost jubilant. Then his tone flattened out, as though remembering he was much too old for summer camp. "Good for them. A little late for me."

"Is there anything else you can tell me about those four boys?" I asked. "Do you have any idea why they would have gone out in that storm?"

"No. Sorry." He let out a sigh. "Camp Stony Owl. I can almost hear the old campfire song. 'Old Stony Owl... stand watchful, noble, and true—'"

He went on a bit, but that was about it for useful information.

"Stacey, guess what I just learned?" I said when I finally got off the phone. Stacey had done one or two more calls herself while I was listening to Trevor talk and sing. And sing.

"That you actually do love camping?" Stacey guessed, and she was way off.

"No. Josh was in Bobcat Cabin. And he was—"

"Best pals with the boys who drowned?"

"Sounds like you've heard it from a second source."

"A third. I guess everyone who was there knew."

"But Josh certainly hasn't mentioned it," I said. "Though he did take it personally when we brought up those three."

"They were his pals. His buds. People said they were a pack. Though bobcats don't form packs, do they?" She frowned. "Prides? That's lions. Bobs? Mobs? That would be cute. A mob of bobcats."

"Still, the guy I talked to had happy memories of camp."

"The lady I talked to said she dreams about it," Stacey said. "Especially as it gets closer to summer."

"Interesting." I stretched and yawned.

One of my voicemails had been from Allison, wanting to set up a time to meet and catch up with us away from her kids. I called back, but she didn't answer. I left a message for her to come by our cabin after nine p.m. if she wanted.

"We'd better catch some sleep while there's daylight left," I told Stacey.

We hiked back to our cabin, where I stretched out on my bunk and closed my eyes.

Not surprisingly, twisted visions of what I'd

experienced in the lodge immediately rose, a bloated dead thing holding me under water that had turned out to be an illusion, perhaps a kind of time slip. I felt again the fingers over my face, how they gripped my mouth and jaw.

Sleep was necessary but rough. My phone alarm came as a relief.

Allison arrived at the cabin's front door with a couple of paper plates covered in aluminum foil. "We had some leftovers," she said. "Just chicken and beans and cole slaw and pie."

"Sounds amazing, thanks!" I set the plates down on the coffee table where Stacey was setting up her laptop. She turned it to face Allison, who sat down on the patched-up thrift-store couch opposite our own.

"Oh, wow." Stacey peeled back the foil, releasing a rich barbecue smell. "This looks so good."

"Maybe we could catch up our client first," I said.

"Go ahead and eat," Allison said. "But what do y'all think about what's going on here?"

"We collected a lot of data from our observation," I said. "I'm sure Josh told you."

"He didn't mention that, no." She was smiling, but her voice had gone tight and tense, like she would have started tearing into Josh if he'd been there and we hadn't. "What did you see?"

"Stacey?"

"Mmm," Stacey replied, her mouth full of baked beans. She put down the plastic fork Allison had provided and tapped at her computer.

"I also had a close encounter in the lodge," I told Allison while Stacey queued things up. "We were up in the attic today and something manifested. It attacked me." I explained as best I could.

"So there really was no water?" Allison asked. "I don't understand."

"If it was Reverend Carmody, it might have been putting some of its memory into me when it touched me," I said. "Replaying the sensations of his death."

"Reverend Carmody, the man who started the camp? How did he die?"

"He drowned. In the bathtub upstairs."

Allison took in a sharp breath. "In the lodge? Carmody's... ghost is stomping around up there?"

"And should be considered dangerous. We think there may be other entities as well, a cluster of them, that sometimes pass through the lodge. They seem mostly interested in the sporting equipment upstairs. We've also observed this cluster out at Bobcat Cabin."

"Really? Josh keeps putting off the restoration of Bobcat. It's his old cabin. I keep telling him we need to get the cabins finished up, too."

Stacey played the clips from Bobcat Cabin—the bunks moving, the peals of invisible laughter.

"That's so disturbing." Allison stared at the screen, her arms wrapped tight around herself. "Why wouldn't Josh have told me this?"

"I can't say for sure, but I'd guess he's very sensitive about the boys who died."

"What?" Her eyes widened in alarm. "What boys?"

"Surely Josh mentioned..." I said, then trailed off.

"Tell me *children* did not die at this camp," Allison said. "Tell me that."

Stacey cringed. I felt like cringing, too.

"We've identified a total of six known deaths on this

property," I said. "Three of them were boys who died while your husband was here."

Allison paled, her mouth open.

"Only because they snuck out," Stacey said. "And went canoeing in a storm. They were taking a lot of risks, and they drowned."

"Three?" She slowly turned her head, looked away out the window, and whispered, "Josh."

"I'm getting the idea you didn't know about any of this." I forced a smile, but my guts were coiling up. I'd suspected Josh might have held the darker parts of the campground's history from her, just as he had from us, but I'd hoped I was wrong.

"I don't know what to think. Are you sure Josh knows about this?" Allison looked like somebody had sucker-punched her, and then sucker-punched her again while she was recovering from that first sucker punch.

"Josh was in the same cabin as the three who died. Apparently he knew them well."

Allison glowered, her green eyes smoldering. In the days I'd known her, I'd never seen her quite like that. "Tell me everything."

We did, filling her in on the history we'd uncovered as well as our own observations. It was all clearly uncomfortable for Allison, so it was uncomfortable for us, too.

After we finished, she sat in silence for a while, staring blankly at the darkness beyond the window.

"We put everything into this place," she said, her voice barely above a whisper. "And it's a death trap. We're ruined."

I felt awful. "I don't know. Maybe we can find the root

of all this."

"Yeah, we'll fix it!" Stacey said, putting on a chipper tone. "Probably. Right, Ellie?"

"We'll see what we dig up," I said, without much certainty. "Everyone we spoke to said this camp was a very positive part of their lives. Except for the, uh, obvious tragic occurrences."

"You really think you can help?" Allison asked me, her eyes pleading.

"We'll do everything we can."

We walked Allison back to the lodge where her SUV was parked, because we were not comfortable letting her go near the lodge alone. She drove away down the gravel road toward her house.

Watching her taillights vanish into the woods, I felt heavy, and not just from the baked beans and the wedge of pecan pie, though I'm sure those contributed. Stacey had a pained look on her face.

"She seemed pretty horrified," Stacey said.

"She should be," I replied, and started back down the trail.

Chapter Twenty-Three

Later, I sat alone in the dark common room of Bobcat
Cabin, my eyes adjusting to the gloom of moonlight
through the windows. It was time to get up close and
personal with the ghosts of Camp Stony Owl.

It was quiet. I could hear my breath, my heartbeat, the
occasional owl outside.

I was on edge, waiting for disembodied laughter or
heavy, thudding footsteps.

Stacey wasn't far away; she was outside on the front
steps of our cabin, listening in via our usual headset
arrangement in case anything decided to kill me or
whatnot. The Bobcat Boys hadn't shown signs of
threatening us before, but they were clearly capable of
shoving a bunk bed at me if they wanted.

Minutes crept by. I triple-checked our cameras and
microphones, the ones in the common room with me as

well as the ones in the bedrooms. I quadruple-checked them. Things stayed quiet.

I thought about Gwendolyn Malloy, the girl who'd allegedly drowned herself going out in a canoe during a storm with her pockets full of rocks. Supposedly an act of grief after finding her fiance and the preacher's wife together.

I still wondered if there was more to the story. For instance, I couldn't rule out the possibility that Gwendolyn had been murdered and someone had made it look like suicide. It was hard to discern a motive—who would have wanted her dead? Why? That train of thought certainly went down a dark tunnel, but without more information it was a dead-end one for now.

Minutes became hours. Midnight slipped by. Then one a.m.

Then the spirits began to stir.

I heard the high-pitched laugh first, then a scraping. Footsteps, like energetic kids running.

"Ellie, I'm hearing things," Stacey said. I tapped my microphone in reply.

As the noises continued, I drew on my thermal goggles.

I felt the wave of cold a moment after I saw the sprawling fog of a cold spot emerge from the hallway.

The entities fell silent, maybe responding to my presence. The coldness moved beyond me and vanished near the door. If my guess was right, these were the Bobcat boys, Josh's old roommates.

Stepping outside, I was able to discern the blue cold front rolling through the cabin area, skirting the fire ring. A half-second of laughter bubbled on the wind.

Stacey's orange and yellow form stepped down from

the cabin. She joined me silently, a warm, orange, living apparition walking beside me on the cool, leafy ground.

We tracked the dead boys in silence.

The lake was their destination, like last time.

At the shore, the fog vanished. Splashes sounded in the water. Maybe it was a creature out on the lake, or maybe the ghosts had gone for a dip in the old-time drowning hole.

Moving closer, I looked out over the vast cool blue of the lake, but couldn't make out any suspicious cold spots.

Stacey tugged my sleeve to grab my attention, then pointed with her glowing yellow fingertip.

A warm, living shape stood in the distance, out on the dock. It looked like Nathan was back for more. If he was calling out any words across the water tonight, they were too distant or low for me to hear.

"He's at it again," I murmured. I scanned back over the lake, looking for any sign of movement, whether a supernatural cold spot or the warm glow of a living person rowing over to meet Nate. Nobody was there, living or dead.

When I looked back at the dock, though, I saw something that made me grab Stacey's arm.

"What?"

"Cold spot. Stay behind me." I began to advance.

This cold spot was qualitatively different from the ones we'd been following. Darker. Denser. Taller. Much taller.

I flashed back to things Allison and Ephraim had mentioned about a tall, strange apparition in their home.

Here it was. It had to be. The thing was treelike in shape, eight or nine feet in height, with strange branching projections at the top.

The shape moved quickly. It was coming from the

direction of Stony Owl, rushing toward the boathouse and dock, its strides inhumanly long and barely touching the ground at all. It was like a hunter closing in on its prey: the person on the dock.

As it moved, it raised an abnormally long arm that ended in a squarish shape, not like a hand at all.

More like the head of an ax, which it lifted as it rushed toward the dock where Nathan stood.

Breaking into a run, I slapped the iPod on my belt. I'd downloaded an assortment of Cherokee music in case of a Trailwalker encounter. The Cherokee had lived in the area many centuries after the lost society that had built Stony Owl, but perhaps there would be some echo of the earlier people. It was the best I had to work with, anyway.

A blast of flutes, rattles, drums, and singing voices filled the air.

I kept running toward the tall shape, flashlight in my hand, ready to strike it with a few thousand lumens.

The shape ceased advancing toward the dock. It turned toward me instead, the strange branch-shapes atop its head towering well above me.

Typically, sacred music is there to ward off the more evil-intentioned sorts of spirits, driving them back from an attack, if not out of the area altogether. It's no guarantee, though, especially when I was missing this particular entity's culture by a couple thousand years.

"Ellie, look," Stacey whispered, her glowing aura staring and pointing. She was seeing it, too, even without enhanced vision.

I lowered my heavy thermal goggles, letting them hang like a brick around my neck.

The apparition ceased its approach when I stopped

mine. It was shadowy, looming over me.

I could see now that the branching shapes that seemed to grow like tree limbs from its head were actually deer antlers, arranged in a high crown and inlaid with beadwork.

The tall apparition wore elaborately arranged animal skins edged with fur and inset with more of the intricate beaded patterns. Woven, beaded skins like heavily decorated boots wrapped her from her knees down to her toes.

She was tall and strong—she'd have to be, to wear that heavy crown—her hair set in serpentine braids, her neck hung with necklaces, her wrists adorned with bangles.

She looked like nothing and no one I'd ever seen before.

Her eyes were solid darkness as she regarded us. Her face showed little expression. It was a difficult gaze to return, so I looked at the long-handled ax in her hands, its stone blade wide and sharp.

A flashlight beam struck us, nearly blinding me. I covered my eyes.

"What's going on?" a male voice asked, his footsteps dashing toward us from the dock. Not Nathan, but Josh. The father and son could easily be mistaken for each other from a distance.

By the time I blinked the glare out of my eyes, the apparition was gone, vanished like a wisp of smoke, like it had never been there at all. It was the kind of thing that could make you question your sanity when you were alone, leaving you wondering if the apparition had been real or in your mind.

"Did you see?" I pointed to where the antler-crowned apparition had been standing. "There was an apparition."

"A ghost?" he asked.

"Yes. She vanished a second ago. I think she was sneaking up on you."

"What did she look like?" Josh had either dropped his former skepticism or was doing an amazing job of pretending to believe me.

I described what I'd seen, with Stacey hopping in to add details. "Do you think it could be the Trailwalker? From the old camp legend?"

"I don't think the legends describe it as a woman." Josh rubbed his chin; he hadn't shaved in a few days and his eyes had dark bags. "Just an old chief. Or warrior."

"Hey, can't a woman be a warrior? Or chief?" Stacey asked.

"Do you know anybody who actually saw the Trailwalker?" I asked.

"It was just a campfire story," he said. "Somebody was going to invent one like it sooner or later, right? I don't know if it was handed down from history or just made up. But I'd bet on the second."

"So you never believed this campground was haunted?"

"I wouldn't say haunted, no. But there is something about this place..." His gaze drifted off, generally toward the lake, but maybe back in time, too. "Maybe there is magic in the old stone owl. We've tried to take care of it. Pulled the weeds, fixed the fence."

Stacey and I shared a look. It was similar to what we'd heard from former campers, those we'd managed to track down.

"Do you mind if I ask what you were doing out here tonight, Josh?" I asked. Stacey cringed a little beside me.

"I could ask you the same thing," he said.

"We tracked a cold spot out here. It emerged back in Bobcat Cabin."

"The Trailwalker did?"

"No. She came from that direction." I pointed toward the Stony Owl hill.

Josh nodded slowly. "Okay."

"Is that why you were here?" I asked. "Did you see something unusual?"

"Me? No, no." He looked toward the lake. "Just dredging up old memories, I guess. Allison's not exactly happy with me right now. I didn't completely fill her in on the history of the place. Well, I just left out one or two of the bad parts. But that stuff's hard for me to talk about."

"Are you sure this place is going to be safe?" I asked. "There's been four drownings."

"Three."

"Before your friends, there was Gwendolyn Malloy. The counselor who drowned here nearly a hundred years ago under the same circumstances. She went paddling in a storm."

"A hundred...well, they probably didn't even use life vests back then. Different times."

"And what about the three boys who drowned when you were here?"

"They didn't wear them, either. They were supposed to, but like I said, they made the worst decisions," he said. "Later on, in college, I had to read *The Odyssey* in this literature class. Those sailors who couldn't resist the siren song, did you read about that? That was Paul, Thomas, and Kyle."

"What siren song?"

"We used to sneak out here to swim late at night," he

said. "Obviously, that was a bad idea, but we were young enough to be invulnerable. The hardest part was getting out of the cabin, sneaking out without the counselor catching you." A dreamy smile slipped over his face. "Good times."

I thought of the cluster of entities arising and making their way from Bobcat Cabin.

"What happened when you snuck out? What did y'all do?"

He gave a crooked smile. "We'd go swimming. Then there was the girl who started showing up. She wasn't even a camper, just a local girl who came swimming at night. Trespassing, I guess, not that we cared. We first met her out here one night—she was watching us from way out in the deep end. Spying on us boys while we wrestled and horsed around in the water. Wait, that's not right. First we *heard* her, then we saw her. She was laughing at us."

"Laughing?" I asked, getting a creepy-crawly feeling up my spine.

"The girl was out near the middle of the lake. She was maybe a couple years older than us, and prettier than any girl I'd ever seen. When you're fifteen, a girl like that can stop your heart. Your brain, too.

"She didn't talk much at first, just laughed and swam away, getting us to chase her out into the deep end. She wore long sleeves and a skirt, which was crazy, but it didn't slow her down. When Matt got close to her over by the Cold Hole, where it felt like winter all year, she went under and didn't come back up.

"We swam all around, looking for her. Kyle was sure she must have drowned. He kept diving down, thinking he'd find her body.

"Then we heard her laughing at us. We couldn't see her,

but she was nearby. Probably hiding behind the bushes on the shore. We didn't see her again that night.

"We snuck out again the next night. She wasn't there at first, but she showed up after a few minutes. Same story. Laughing at us. Teasing us, coming closer, then slipping away underwater before anyone could catch her. She tagged Matt from behind once, scared him straight up out of the water. He yelled out." Josh shook his head. "We snuck out a couple times. She wasn't always there. She kept us guessing."

"What happened the final night?" I asked, trying to be as delicate as possible.

"It was raining," Josh said, and all traces of a smile left his face. "She came to the window. Kyle heard her first. He was always quieter than us. Better at listening, I guess. So he hears tapping. *Tap tap tap*, like that. He was the first to walk over there. She was looking in at us, soaking wet—I mean, it was really coming down. A storm was brewing.

"Kyle opens the window, thinking she's going to come in, but he can't get the screen off. She just stands there smiling like she's got the best secret to tell.

"She wouldn't come in. Instead she challenged us to a race. She said the first boy to catch her would get a kiss.

"Well, the others ran for the door, and she laughed watching them scramble at her words. I was still in my bunk, though. Left in the room alone. She was watching me with a smile, and I was embarrassed because I was in my underwear, which was why I hadn't left my bunk yet. I didn't want to take my sheet off while she was watching.

"Then lightning flashed, a big sheet of lightning that turned night to day for about a second.

"For that second, she looked different to me. Maybe it

was my imagination, or a trick of the light, or me being sleepy and half-dreaming, but when she was all lit up, she changed.

"She looked... scary. Like, did you ever see *Swamp Thing*? Or maybe *Night of the Living Dead*? She looked like a cross between those. Like something that crawled out of a wet grave. She was all covered in mud. Her face was distorted somehow. Discolored. I could have sworn mud was leaking from her nose and mouth. She looked like a dead person standing out there.

"Then the lightning faded and she was normal again, a pretty girl in the rain, but she wasn't smiling anymore. It was like she knew what I'd seen.

"I heard the guys yelling outside, and she was gone in an eyeblink. The same way she used to disappear underwater while we played. Nobody could ever catch her.

"I ran out after the guys. They had a big head start; they were already past the bathhouse, running toward the trail to the lake. I yelled after them to wait, but the rain was really pounding down. Wind, thunder. They couldn't hear me. Even if they could, I doubt they would have stopped.

"So I followed. By the time I caught up, they were already at the lake. The light in the boathouse was on. The guys came running out with a canoe.

"I asked where they were going, and they just pointed, because even up close we could barely hear each other in the storm.

"The lake looked like I'd never seen it, choppy like an ocean, waves crashing against the dock and the shore. I couldn't believe the guys were even thinking about going out there.

"I saw her in another flash of lightning. She was in a

canoe of her own, already yards out from shore. She was standing up in it, gripping the top lip with her bare feet; the storm was whipping up the lake, rocking her boat side to side, but she smiled and waved like all was fine. Surfing the storm in an old wooden canoe. Her clothes were wet and sagging off her, and she looked more gorgeous than ever.

"The guys pretty much went crazy when they saw her, I mean they were like mindless dogs, and they charged out into the water. I didn't go with them, because of what I'd seen earlier. But I couldn't stop them. I didn't really know what to say. I didn't... I should have tried harder." Josh swallowed hard. "They paddled out, and I never saw them again. I found a flashlight in the boathouse, and I saw their canoe overturned.

"I ran all the way back to our cabin and woke up our counselor. And that was the end of it." Josh wasn't looking at us at all, but out at the lake where it had all happened. "By the time they pulled the guys out of the lake, it was all over. They didn't find the girl or her boat. I don't know what happened to her."

I was filled with suspicions and ideas about the girl, but I wasn't sure where to start with them. "I'm sorry. That must have been terrible."

"Yeah." Finally he looked at me, his face hardening. "And that's why I don't like the idea of the guys playing a part in your ghost story."

"But do you think there could be anything unusual happening here at the campground?" I asked. "Even if you're not willing to say it's haunted—"

"I wasn't wrong, was I?" His expression softened, becoming almost vulnerable, a glimpse of a scared person beneath his mask of salesman bravado. "What I saw in the flash of lightning. When she looked like a monster. Do you think that was real?"

"It sounds likely."

"So what was she?" Josh shivered a little. "Was she a... you know.... was she something unnatural the whole time?"

"It's possible you were seeing an apparition of Gwendolyn Malloy, the girl who died here in the camp's first incarnation," I said. "What you've described about her appearance and her clothing fit, too. Of course, we can't be sure—"

"Why would she want to kill us?" Josh asked.

"Maybe she wanted some friends to play with," Stacey suggested. "We've seen that before. The dead can get lonely."

"They do seem to come out of the cabin and travel the campground at night," I said. "And we've heard laughter. High-pitched laughter."

"She laughed a lot," Josh said. "More than she talked, really. When she talked, she was usually daring us to do something."

"Gwendolyn died the same way your friends did," I said. "That could mean she was repeating her own death by drowning them. Or it could mean some underlying cause, something older, was behind all of these deaths."

"The Trailwalker," Josh said, his voice hushed. "Do you think... maybe they used to do human sacrifice or something out here?"

"Well, I hadn't thought of that—"

"That was another legend. More of a rumor, really. Probably as made up as the rest, though."

"But we saw the Trailwalker," Stacey said.

"Yet we don't really know anything about her," I said.

"Anything is possible. Josh, if your friends are still here, I don't think they are malevolent. I don't believe they would mean us harm. But they may be under the control of something more powerful."

Josh was quiet, his eyes on the water. "I keep dreaming about them. All my life, really, but especially since we moved back here. I see them out in the water, waiting. There's an empty place in the group. The place where I belong." He sighed. "Maybe I should drown myself in the lake. Allison's ready to kill me now that she knows."

"You had to know she'd find out eventually," Stacey said.

"Well, once it was up and running, and had passed every safety inspection..." Josh shook his head. "That's what I've been telling myself. That eventually it'll be fine. The past is the past. I just wanted to... feel the way I used to feel when I was a kid, I guess. Stupid now that I say it out loud." He looked around the little village of freshly restored activity centers. "I guess it's over."

I couldn't help feeling pity for him, watching him sag like that. He looked a decade older than he was, going gray at the edges. "Even if the campground doesn't open, you should let us continue until we resolve what's happening here. To free your friends and any other souls trapped here. To end the haunting, if we can."

"Yeah. Of course. You really think the guys are still here, then?"

"I do," I said. "Have you really not seen anything since moving here? No hint of a ghost?"

He shook his head. "I wish I had. I wish I'd seen the guys again. That's what I think about when I come down here to the dock. But all I see are my own memories."

"That's what ghosts are, in a way," I said. "Some are stronger and clearer than others. Pieces of broken souls that haven't fully moved on. Did you know your son's been coming down here alone at night, too?"

"Ephraim?"

"Nathan. He says he sometimes meets a local girl here."

"Yeah, that would be Nate. What girl?"

"After what you've told me, I'm concerned it's the same one you saw," I said. "Gwendolyn's ghost, luring him down here."

"He hasn't said anything about this."

"Nathan comes out later than you do," I said. "I've warned him to stay away from the lake, but he's not listening to me. You should tell him. He might try again tonight."

Josh nodded. "I'll do that. So what's next? Can you really change things around here?"

"I have some ideas." That was an exaggeration—I had one idea. But I wanted to reassure him. "We'll stick around until we figure it out. In the meantime, keep your family members away from the lake. Especially alone, and especially at night."

Chapter Twenty-Four

"You've certainly had me digging into quite the basket of small-town dirty laundry, my dear," Grant Patterson said, bright and very early the next morning.

Stacey and I had pretty much gone to ground for the rest of the previous night, hiding in our cabin with the doors and windows locked and latched, every window curtain drawn. We'd even traded off some sleeping time, not that it did me much good—my dreams had been full of dark things walking through the woods, of dead things crawling on the slimy mud floor of the lake.

Grant was now calling back with some information wrangled from the university's records.

"Do you mind if I put you on speaker so Stacey can hear?" I asked. Stacey yawned and gave me a thumbs up.

"Of course not. Who could resist the delightful sense of conversing from the bottom of an echoing well?"

"Great, thanks." I grabbed my notepad. "Now let's unload that dirty laundry."

"Terrance Baker," Grant said. "After graduating, he went on to law school at the University of Tennessee and joined a small firm in Chattanooga. Later, in August of 1939, Mr. Baker was caught in an indelicate situation with the wife of a judge. This particular gentleman was known locally as 'Hangman' Harry O'Shannon and was quite the fan of firearms and, we might surmise, of summary vigilante justice as well as the death penalty for adultery, for he passed and carried out that very sentence upon Mr. Terrance Baker upon discovering him in the midst of the, well, scandalous behavior.

"Despite his moniker, Hangman O'Shannon performed the deed with a revolver, in his own bedroom, leaving his own sheets bloody and bullet-riddled while his straying wife screamed in the corner. The judge had no trouble convincing his friend and golf partner, the prosecutor, that he was acting in self-defense, believing he'd encountered an intruder in his home, and the case was buried as quickly as Terrance's corpse."

"So Terrance *was* a total snake," Stacey said. "He cheated on Gwendolyn with the preacher's wife when he was a camp counselor, then he had an affair with a judge's wife when he was a lawyer."

"He does seem to have been quite the legless reptilian regarding intimate relationships," Grant agreed.

"What happened to the judge's wife?" I asked.

"They remained married until the Hangman's death forty years later. Apparently the incident proved only a brief hiccup in their marriage."

"Amazing," Stacey said. "You have to admire a strong

relationship like that."

Grant sent us a photograph of Terrance—smiling, handsome, despite a small scar at his jawline.

After that, Grant told us about Gwendolyn Malloy, mostly things we already knew—grew up in Valdosta, made high grades, never finished college because of her death.

"As for the preacher's disappearing wife, I may have lucked into something as well," he continued. "If we assume she reverted to Laurie Ann Wilkerson after self-liberating from her husband, then it seems likely she died in 1947, age fifty-two. Lung cancer. I forwarded her obituary to you; it mentions no spouse or children. She was the evening shift manager at Lumpy's Burgers in Tallapoosa, Georgia, an independent establishment specializing in American diner cuisine."

"That really fills in a lot of blanks for us," I said. "Thanks, Grant."

"Have you seen Stony Owl in person?"

"Sure have."

"Remarkable. It was clearly the burial place of a highly respected individual. The placing of a stone on a grave when one passes is a sign of respect in many cultures. Great mounds of stones may indicate the presence of a grand personality indeed, one remembered for many generations after his death."

"Or hers," I said, thinking of the towering apparition with the antler crown.

"Naturally. Do you have any particular reason to believe a female leader is buried at Stony Owl? That would be a tantalizing discovery."

"I think I may have seen her," I said.

"Fantastic! That must be an old ghost indeed. What did

she look like?"

I tried my best to describe her—tall, her eyes large and dark, her face stern, her arms strong. Grant drank in every detail, down to the beadwork, and I'm pretty sure he was taking notes.

When I finally extricated myself from that phone call, I told Stacey it was time to get moving.

"I thought it was time for second sleep," she complained.

"It's to make a road trip," I said. "Wear something you don't mind getting a little dirty."

"Sounds exciting," Stacey said. "Can we get breakfast first, dirty second?"

"That's probably a good order to do it in," I said.

We had breakfast at a spot in Blairsville called Cook's Country Kitchen. Then it was time to go "grave diving"—a term Stacey used, not me.

We drove to the nearby Owltown Cemetery, a small, pastoral sort of place, no fence or walls, just some scattered trees for shade.

The preacher had an economy-class grave marker, a little concrete rectangle on the ground offering the least amount of information it could without actually being blank: CARMODY 1929. Nobody had lavished money on that one. While many of the graves were new enough to have fresh flowers from visitors, Reverend Carmody's grave lay forgotten under a juniper tree whose base had widened enough to almost cover the marker. Dandelions and wildflowers grew around the marker's edges.

"Here we are, but what about the guy?" Stacey nodded at the gardener; we'd been unlucky enough to show up while the graveyard was being mowed. The guy had a wagon full of tools, too, like he expected to do some up-close trimming and weeding afterward, really making a day of it.

"He doesn't look like he's going anywhere for a while," I said.

We were here to collect soil from Carmody's grave, but the gardener, a portly, sweaty man in his mid-fifties, kept squinting at us from under his straw hat. He could surely tell we were from out of town and seemed unsure as to whether he cared for our presence in his domain of the dead. He probably thought we were up to something suspicious. He wasn't wrong.

"Okay, you kneel there and block his view," I whispered.

Stacey nodded. We got into position, then waited for the gardener to turn his back to us as he started mowing in the opposite direction. There was nothing to stop him from looking over his shoulder, though, to check whether we were trying to desecrate the little graveyard. Which we kind of were, but only a little bit.

As soon as he turned away, I brought out a small mason jar and a plastic spoon from Cook's Country Kitchen. A trowel would have been more convenient and much faster, but we don't typically carry gardening supplies in the van. Shovels, sometimes, but not trowels.

"Ugh," I grunted, fighting tough, hard-packed soil. I scraped up earth from around the edges of Carmody's marker, hacking clover and tiny wildflowers at the roots.

The lawnmower stopped abruptly.

"Are you sure you're blocking me?" I whispered. Stacey squatted on the other side of the marker from me; behind her, I could see the gardener. He walked toward us, brushing his gloves together to knock off dirt and grass clippings. He was coming much too fast—not running, but he had a long stride, so he could possibly walk at a slow gait yet still manage to outrun us, like Jason from the *Friday the 13th* movies.

"Let's go." I stood up quickly. I couldn't really hide the jar—it was a warm day and I wasn't wearing my jacket. When I jammed the plastic spoon into my jeans pocket, the head of it snapped off and fell to the ground. I hurried to grab it up so we wouldn't leave litter behind, which delayed us further.

"What are y'all up to over here?" the gardener asked, striding closer like an undead serial killer who was totally confident his victims could never outrun him.

"Heading out," I said, backing away.

"What's in your hand?" He pointed at the jar. Then he looked down at the grave marker and scowled, instantly seeing the spoon-width trench I'd dug alongside it. His eye for detail was getting us in trouble. "What kinda devilry is this?"

"We were just, uh, you know..." I struggled to think of a story, then said, "Running away."

We turned and bolted toward the van.

We clambered inside. I couldn't get the van started, even as the graveyard gardener advanced toward us, glaring, rapidly covering the distance between us with his long, deliberate, murderous strides. Okay, maybe they weren't really "murderous" but it felt that way in the moment.

Finally, the van's engine sputtered to life. I stepped on the gas and we were off. In my sideview, I saw the gardener step out into the road, watching us depart with a glowering look on his face.

"Well, that's one more graveyard we can never come back to." Stacey took the jar from the cupholder where I'd placed it. "You think Carmody will respond to his own burial earth?"

"Sometimes they do, sometimes they don't. But the only personal possessions of his we can find will be in the lodge he already haunts, so those probably won't serve as much of a lure, either. Using an entity's burial earth might be pretty much an act of desperation, but here we are." I put on speed, as much as the lethargic old van would allow. We still had much to do before nightfall.

Chapter Twenty-Five

Night fell. I thought I could smell rain in the air, but the forecast didn't call for any. Maybe it was just the natural mugginess of the campground.

Stacey and I sat out in the van, monitoring the interior of the lodge. We'd set up the stamper in the most obvious spot, the attic bathroom where the preacher had died in the tub. It seemed to be his main lair.

The ghost trap was baited with the dirt, clover, and tiny wildflowers that had been growing from Carmody's grave. To try to increase his potential interest in the trap, we'd added a picture from downstairs, a cataract-yellow photograph of Reverend Carmody and Laurie Ann in their campaign hats and khaki uniforms. A small candle burned near the top of the trap, which sometimes helped lure entities closer.

Nothing happened for a long time.

"Okay, so if he does take the bait, it'll be good when Carmody's ghost isn't clomping around anymore, but then what?" Stacey asked while we waited. "Will we try to trap Gwen and the three boys, too? Catch and release?"

"Possibly, but that'll be difficult. It would be better to help them move on, but that means we have to go deeper. Confront the underlying thing that's binding them here."

"The Trailwalker."

"She's one candidate."

"But Ellie, if the Trailwalker's a thousand years old, and she's taken several lives that we know of... wouldn't that mean she's taken a lot of them over the years?" Stacey fidgeted, uncomfortable, but such was the seating in the back of the van. "That's a lot of time. And if she has that many souls—"

"Then she's powerful. And dangerous."

We chewed on that quietly for a while. The entity had certainly been impressive, a tall and powerful warrior armed with an ax, her feet wrapped in decorative leather that must have enabled her to stalk silently through the wilderness, hunting men or beasts.

Nothing stirred around the lodge except the cackling, hooting owls.

I jumped when my phone rang at one in the morning. The phone number was the landline for the caretaker's cottage.

"Hello?" I said, not sure who to expect.

"I saw it again." Allison sounded out of breath, panicky. "It was here."

"What did you see?"

"It walked through my window again. The tall one. Like a tree."

"The Trailwalker. It's in your house now?"

"No. I got up and followed it. I was scared, but my kids... Anyway, it walked past Shiloh's room, and past the boys, too. I lost sight of it. Then I saw it out the window, walking away down the trail." She swallowed. "Toward the campground. Toward y'all. So keep an eye out."

"Okay. Thanks for the warning. Everybody's okay there? You checked on all three kids? Nobody's outside?" I was mostly worried that Nathan might be out wandering.

"The kids are fine."

"Great. Thanks again. Are you going to be okay?"

She sighed. "I don't know. I won't be going back to sleep anytime soon."

It wasn't long before the paranormal activity started in the lodge.

We'd been focused on the ghost trap upstairs, with its candle flame dancing and beckoning. After such a quiet night, we were startled when the first crash sounded over the speaker.

"The museum," Stacey whispered, pointing to another monitor. The pedestal displaying the old stuffed owl had toppled over, rupturing the owl within; feathers and talons and glass were scattered all around. The dead owl wasn't much of a loss in itself, but whatever entity had pushed it possessed a dangerous level of psychokinetic energy.

"Check the footage," I said. Stacey pulled up the museum camera's last few minutes on her tablet.

In the greenish monochrome hues of night vision, something skimmed past the dead owl display—a tiny, spherical orb, not much bigger than a marble, or a fingertip. The pedestal went crashing over. The orb continued on toward the archaeological section.

Another crash sounded, this one over the real-time feed from the museum. On the live monitor, the top of the archaeological display had buckled, as though someone had struck it with a heavy invisible object. Like an ax.

Glancing back at the ghost trap upstairs, I saw no activity at all.

"I want a closer look." I opened the door and dropped out of the van, even as a third smash rang out from the monitors.

"It's not safe in there!" Stacey protested.

"That's why we're using the buddy system tonight. Come on."

"Oh, right. Buddy system." Stacey hopped out and followed me to the lodge.

The lodge was chilly when we stepped through the front door. It only grew colder as we approached the museum.

From inside the museum's closed door, we heard more banging and crashing.

"Okay," I whispered. "Let's have a look."

I opened the door.

Inside, the archaeological portion of the display shuddered as though a tiny earthquake trembled beneath it. Another invisible blow buckled the top of the display case buckled in another spot. The Plexiglas front of the display wobbled and vibrated as though something was pounding it repeatedly. It didn't shatter, though, which probably frustrated the unseen entity.

A deep gouge appeared above the display, hacking into the wall Josh had only recently replaced and painted after finding it clawed to pieces, like so much of the lodge's interior.

Another gouge ruptured the wall, and then a third, a fourth. The gouges looked as Allison had described the earlier damage, like the claw mark of a large bear. They appeared in quick succession, as if hacked by someone lashing out in frustration and anger, possibly trying to bring the ceiling down on all of us.

The front of the display vibrated so much that the artifacts inside—the obsidian blade, the copper owl—blurred as the Plexiglas in front of them wobbled like a guitar string.

An angry howl pierced the air, barely human, an expression of frustration and fury.

I took Stacey by the arm and silently led her back and away from the museum to the big main room with the fireplace.

"That's pretty weird," Stacey whispered. She nodded back toward the museum as more crashing and howling sounded.

"Yep." I called Allison back on the landline. She picked up instantly.

"What's happening?" she asked.

"I believe the Trailwalker's back at the lodge. It's smashing the place up all over again. Can you tell me where to find the keys to the museum displays?"

"My desk, top drawer on the left. Why?"

"I'm trying to calm it down." I ran to the office, then back to the little museum, Stacey at my back the whole time.

The museum had fallen silent and still, the destruction ceased. I didn't think the entity had left, though—it was freezing cold in there, and I had a definite feeling of being watched as I tiptoed through the open doorway, gripping the keys like I was planning to use them as a weapon. Not that stabbing a ghost with a key would have any effect, unless maybe that particular ghost had a powerful emotional tie to that particular key.

The archaeological display had taken the brunt of the entity's fury. The wall above it was damaged in a dozen places, and the top of the display had been splintered and broken.

The Plexiglas front panes still held, though they dangled loosely from damaged hinges.

Cautiously, I knelt on the floor, inserted the key into one of the locked panes and turned.

"Ell..." Stacey's voice rushed out in a loud whisper, but she didn't need to say anything at all. I saw it.

The dark shadow towered over us, ten or eleven feet tall with the branching antlers at the top, a profile more like a tree than a human. She might have been exaggerating her size; such things as size and appearance can be quite malleable to ghosts.

If her intent was to strike fear, it was working. I could feel my heart jackhammering inside my chest as I looked up at the cold, dark, featureless shadow figure. It seemed to suck all the air, heat, and light out of the room.

"You..." I could barely speak. I swallowed, trying to catch my breath in the suddenly thin and cold air. I made myself speak to the ancient entity. "You want your things back. Right?"

It did not respond.

"Okay. Reasonable enough." Slowly, I eased open the front panel. It was supposed to swing open like a door, but two of its three hinges had been broken, so it just sort of dropped aside and hung there, crooked and loose.

I reached in and withdrew a banglwedding ringe studded with little seashells.

As I set it on the floor, the room turned colder.

I removed one ancient item after another, laying them at the shadow figure's feet like a vassal paying tribute to an empress. An obsidian blade. A stone ax head. The silver piece etched with a simple beaver-or-badger design, the bronze plate with the owl scratched into it.

When I'd set them all out, I crawled backward on my hands and knees, obsequious as a peasant before a pharaoh, before finally standing. Stacey was close by my side. I could see her frosty breath in the dim room, illuminated only by light leaking in from the hallway outside.

I checked to make sure I'd set out each item and nothing remained in the display case.

"Okay?" I whispered, trembling, looking at the dark shape. "Those are yours. I understand. We can return them to the owl. We'll bury them for you."

The shadow-shape became more distinct, easing forward, and again we saw the fierce warrior woman, crowned in antlers, carrying an ax that strongly resembled the stone ax head from the case. Her version looked freshly polished and sharpened along its cutting edge, and decorated with paint.

The entity held out an empty hand, palm down.

On the floor, the artifacts trembled, moved by invisible ripples of psychokinetic energy.

Her face was stoic, her large black eyes like painted rocks. She had not been alive in many, many centuries. She had the stillness of the long dead.

Then her expression twisted into a mask of fury, teeth bared, lips curling back.

An ear-splitting howl of rage filled the room.

She vanished.

Then it was like a bomb exploded. Shelves were blasted off the walls. The nature displays tore loose from their wall mounts and crashed to the floor. Light bulbs burst overhead.

"We're out!" I screamed. Stacey and I bolted for the door and slammed it shut behind us, just as a rain of shattered glass and broken beads clattered against it.

We ran through the lodge and didn't stop until we were outside, leaning against the familiar shape of the van, catching our breath, completely shocked.

"Okay," I said. "That could have gone a lot better."

My phone rang. Allison again, no doubt wanting an update.

I took a deep breath, not quite sure how to explain what had just happened.

Chapter Twenty-Six

"This is even worse than when we first got here," Josh said the next morning. He and Allison had come to survey the museum damage, leaving the boys to watch Shiloh. We had advised them to stay home and away from the lodge until daylight, and we'd taken that advice for ourselves, too.

It looked like a whirlwind had torn through the museum, smashing everything. Deep, long ax marks covered the walls and floor as if some giant beast had clawed up the room.

"We have it all on video," I said, hanging back in the doorway with Stacey.

"I'll have to start all over," Josh murmured.

"I thought she might be after the grave goods she'd been buried with." I pointed to the artifacts arranged on the floor where I'd left them. "But it just sent her into a wilder fury, if anything. She clearly has an opinion about them, I'll say that."

"I can't believe we're stuck with this awful place," Allison murmured, staring at the broken, dead owl in its case, its feathers everywhere.

"It's not *awful*—" Josh began, but she cut him off with a severe look. Allison, not surprisingly, was still seething over Josh not mentioning the deaths at the camp before they'd bought it.

"So, on the bright side, something triggered our trap upstairs while we were distracted with all the big events downstairs," I told them.

"Yeah, we even caught a cold spot heading that way!" Stacey was extra chipper, as if she could will the mood in the room to lighten up. She couldn't, though. "So we probably captured one. Possibly. Y'all want to see the video?"

"You actually trapped a ghost?" Josh asked, either genuinely interested or eager to turn the conversation away from his own mistakes. "Can I see it?"

"There's not much to see..." I unzipped my backpack where I'd stashed the ghost trap after inspecting the stamper. Carmody's picture and grave earth were inside, the bits of clover and wildflowers shriveled and brown. Josh peered into the cylindrical trap. I answered his questions briefly, explaining the thick leaded glass and electromagnetic field that worked together to keep the entity inside, at least until the battery died.

Allison watched from a distance, her face set into a glower, a detonation waiting for a trigger. I did my best to avoid providing one.

"We can help you clean up," I said. "Since I couldn't stop the entity."

"You don't have to do that," Josh said.

"Oh, no, we totally insist." Stacey drew on gloves. I'd put mine on, too, before returning to the wrecked room.

I walked over to the epicenter of damage, the destroyed archaeological display, the wall above so thick with overlapping hack-marks it almost looked like the Trailwalker had tried to write a message. Or maybe the logo of a heavy metal band.

"I really don't understand," I said. "I thought she wanted her stuff. What's that?"

Josh and Stacey stepped closer to see where I pointed.

"I don't know," Josh said, barely above a whisper.

Kneeling, I pulled off splintered, broken pieces of what had been the wooden floor of the archaeological display case. The little mound of quartzite rocks taken from the Stony Owl effigy had been heaped there in a tiny imitation of the effigy; now they were scattered across the room or had fallen through the ax-damaged base.

The damage to the display's floor revealed its base was hollow. Pulling off the broken bits and lengths of wood, I revealed what had been hidden within: a rust-splotched iron box, locked at the front.

"What is that?" Allison hurried over to join us. "Josh, what is that?"

"I don't know," he said. "I didn't know anything was inside there."

"There's no opening or access panel in the base. Whoever put this here meant to keep it concealed for the long term." I brushed quartzite pebbles off the box.

After some trial and error with the museum key ring, I found the key to the box.

"I'm not sure I want to see what's in there," Allison

said, suddenly looking ill.

"Maybe you don't," I said, but she didn't look away.

The lock resisted, turning slowly. It wasn't just the outside of the iron box that had gone rusty over the years.

Right when I thought I'd have to go grab my lock picks, the lock gave with a reluctant hiss, as though I'd awoken a serpent inside.

"Okay," I said, positioning my gloved fingers on the front corners. "Let's just... get it over with."

I lifted the lid.

Allison screamed. Josh recoiled with a grunt like he'd been punched in the stomach, then let out a series of hacking sounds; for a minute I thought he would throw up, adding fresh biohazards to the significant mess already present in the room.

Stacey flinched and drew in a long, sharp breath between her teeth.

I suppose I wasn't as shocked; my intuition about what we'd find had been right, unfortunately.

Broken pieces of bone were scattered inside, along with chunks of deer antler inset with heavy beadwork.

Most notable, though, was the dirt-colored human skull at the center of the box, almost certainly the one amateur archaeologist Tennyford was holding in the yellowed photograph that had been knocked from the back of the display, its frame shattered.

"Oh," Stacey said. "Well, if that's her head, there's a good chance she's going to want that back."

"Agreed." I closed the box in a hurry.

"So... should we put the bones into a trap? Try to nab the Trailwalker?" Stacey asked.

I thought it over. "No. Let's gather up all this stuff

from her grave and return it where it belongs. Today, before sunset. Right now, in fact." I looked at Josh. "I hope you guys have some shovels."

Looking at the rusty box, he nodded slowly, still reeling from the sight of the skull.

Chapter Twenty-Seven

A thick fog had risen in the mountains, so we couldn't see more than a few steps ahead. It was like walking through a dream, clouds obscuring every side. The trees were shadowy sentinels, watching us intruders in this land where perhaps none of us belonged, this ancient site of unknown purpose. Perhaps Tennyford had been right, and there had been an entire temple complex here, a forgotten holy city from a forgotten world.

Stacey and I hiked the steep, winding trail toward the effigy mound along with the entire Conner family. The boys trudged behind, carrying shovels and spades, as happy as any pair of teenagers recruited into heavy manual labor first thing in the morning.

Shiloh held her mother's hand, watching the foggy wilderness with wide eyes, saying nothing.

The wooded hillside was unusually quiet; the owls and

bats had gone for the day, but the morning birds seemed to slumber on in the deep fog, untouched by sunlight. Or maybe only night creatures lived on Stony Owl Hill.

Josh opened the gate and led us inside. We were as quiet as a funeral procession, which I supposed was appropriate for our purpose there.

With so much fog, we couldn't see most of the enormous mound of rocks even when we stood beside it. The place had a definite graveyard feel, like it was full of unseen presences, watching from all around, just out of sight. We kept our voices low, instinctively, the way one does in the presence of the dead.

"Where, Ellie?" Allison asked.

"Charles Tennyford dug a trench to the owl's heart," I said. "So we should bury it in the center."

"That's the thickest part, though," Ephraim said.

"It'll take forever," Nathan added, in case we hadn't caught Ephraim's subtext.

"Then it's a good thing we're starting early." Josh picked up a shovel and stepped onto the stone pile.

"Wait," I told him, then nodded at Stacey.

She set up the speakers we normally carried on our belts. Over them we played a list of assorted Cherokee music—still off by at least a thousand years or more, but the Trailwalker had seemed to respond to it. Hopefully, it conveyed our positive intent, if nothing else.

"Keep your eyes open," I said. "Remember, Tennyford died here."

"But there's no more mountain lions now," Ephraim said. "Unless you're saying..."

"He was also camping here at night, right by the big burial mound," Nathan said.

"No way I would ever do that," Ephraim said.

"Yeah, cause you're a pluckin' chicken." Nathan snorted.

"Watch your language, Nathan!" Allison snapped.

"I did. All I said was Effie's a—"

"Nathan!" She cut him off.

"Don't call me Effie," Ephraim added.

"Stacey, you stick with Allison and Shiloh," I said. "Stay off the rocks and near the gate. I'll stay close to these guys and keep watch. For friendly animals," I added, for Shiloh's benefit, but she looked at me with obvious doubt. The kid knew a lie when she heard one.

As the grumbling teenagers began to dig, I went on a slow patrol around the mound. Even with my flashlight, I couldn't see far through the fog.

I listened for footsteps, watched for shadow figures, took EMF and temperature readings. The bones and other items had to be returned to the grave, I was sure, but it was possible the Trailwalker wouldn't appreciate us digging here regardless.

Tense, on edge, I expected an attack from any direction. The hilltop could certainly have picked a better morning to be sheathed in heavy fog and deep shadows.

Josh and the boys dug and dug, lifting and dropping, the blades of their shovels scraping against quartzite.

Allison kept close to her daughter, who played silently with plastic late-model Disney heroines I didn't even recognize. Shiloh concentrated so intensely on the little figures that I thought her eyes might burn a hole through them, a look I'd seen on her mother's face before. Her lips moved as she walked them through the weeds and dirt, but she didn't say anything I could hear.

Drawing close to the old observation tower, I gazed up at the viewing gallery at the top, from which Stacey and I had gazed down on the owl in its full glory. I wondered if the ancients had built a similar tower in their day, or perhaps climbed nearby trees for the complete view.

The Mississippian mound builder culture had been a civilization spanning thousands of miles when Hernando de Soto and friends arrived with the diseases that destroyed them. The hill where we stood might well have been an active temple complex or home to a powerful chieftain around the time the Caesars had ruled Rome. Unfortunately, there were no records of any of it. Just bowls, blades, and bones.

"Shiloh!" Allison called. "Shiloh, slow down!"

I hurried toward her voice, but it was hard to see what was happening. As I drew closer, I saw Stacey's beam cutting through the fog. Stacey was chasing Allison, who chased Shiloh, who was running toward the open gate.

"Shiloh, we're staying together, honey!"

"But there's people in the woods," Shiloh said, in her small voice. She pointed through the gate to the fog-thick woods beyond.

"Let's stay back from the woods and inside the fence, everyone!" Stacey said.

"What kind of people, Shiloh?" I asked, startling everyone. Great, now I was the creepy shadow suddenly emerging from the fog.

"I don't know," she answered, staring out the gate to the woods.

"What are they doing?"

"Watching us. Not smiling. They must be cold. It's cold today."

"It sure is." I shared a concerned look with Stacey, then turned back to the mound. "Guys, that's probably deep enough."

I hurried toward the mound, unzipping my backpack.

"They're coming closer," Shiloh said, her voice fearful yet sing-songy at the same time.

"Stacey, bring everyone this way! Everyone stay together!" I said as I reached the mound of rocks. Josh, Ephraim, and Nathan had paused their digging to look at me.

"What's happening?" Josh said.

"We need to hurry." I looked out at the fog; I couldn't see much beyond where Stacey, Allison, and Shiloh huddled together, barely visible themselves, like ghosts in a cloud. Stacey had her flashlight widened into floodlight mode, trying to create a protective shield of white light against any advancing spirits, for whatever that was worth.

The guys had only managed to dig down a few feet into the rocks. We should have gone much deeper, down into the soil below the mound, where everything had originally been buried.

But we were out of time.

Shapes appeared in the fog all around the owl effigy mound. Tall, spindly shadow-shapes—if we'd been in the woods, I would have assumed they were small trees, barely glimpsed through the fog, their twig-thin limbs reaching out like arms.

But no trees of that size grew inside the fence, and these shapes had not been there a moment earlier.

"Mommy!" Shiloh screamed, no longer sing-songy, burying her face in her mother's sleeve.

"What's going on?" Ephraim asked.

"We've attracted some paranormal attention." I knelt next to the little pit they'd dug, wishing it was much deeper. Then I opened my backpack.

We had transferred everything out of the rusty iron box since it was obviously not original to the grave. Perhaps Tennyford had stored the remains in it after his excavation in the 1800s. The skull and bones of the Trailwalker had been missing from her grave for more than a century, if so.

It was unusual for a spirit to hang around for thousands of years, but it seemed the Trailwalker had not been a typical person, nor this mound a typical settlement.

The artifacts were in a burlap bag, which I set carefully down into the hole.

The ground shifted beneath us with a low rumble.

Not the ground—the rocks, the million tiny rocks that made up the mound, had begun to shift and slide, as though the earth below had turned to quicksand. Or maybe something was trying to climb out of the grave below. Something enormous.

"Get off!" I shouted at the guys. "Everybody off!"

"Why should we—" Nathan began, but his father forced him off the stone owl. Ephraim ran off the owl without being told.

Everybody grouped together, off to one side of the owl.

Everybody except me, kneeling in the rocks that had begun to shift this way and that.

My backpack, still holding the Trailwalker's bones, slid away as I reached for it. The moving rocks carried it downhill and off toward the Stony Owl's wing.

Grunting in frustration, I crawled after it on hands and knees, sharp rocks jabbing me everywhere as the thousands of rocks of the burial mound kept moving and sliding. I lost my balance and face-planted, taking some stinging rocks to the face.

Stacey swung her light back and forth as more and more of the tall, string-thin dark shapes appeared in the fog —not just one entity, but a group of them, maybe spirits as old as the Trailwalker herself. Perhaps there was more than one grave on this mound. Maybe there were many bodies buried here. Or maybe this was her entourage, her bodyguards, whatever loyal servants she might have had in life, still loyally serving her in death.

Our iPod died and the Cherokee music stopped, removing whatever protection it might have afforded us, if any.

In the trees all around, the owls hooted up a storm, awoken from their morning slumber by all the noise. If owls were said to guide the dead to the next world, perhaps they could also guide souls back from the land of the dead, under the right circumstances; owls awake and chattering in the daytime, a reversal of the normal, natural order, just as the dead returning to our world was a reversal. These were the kind of fevered thoughts my mind was generating at the time.

I stretched out on my stomach and managed to hook a finger around one strap of my backpack before it slid completely out of reach.

A massive column of solid darkness towered over me, taller than ever, swallowing all the light. Perhaps the fog turned thicker and grayer, or clouds had drawn across the rising sun like a cloak, but the world went dark as night in her presence, as if even the heavens bowed to her authority.

I was freezing cold and isolated—Stacey and the family

could have been a thousand miles away, for all that I could see or hear them. Maybe it was a trick of the fog, too. Or a trick of the supernatural, moving me away from the rules of the regular world into places I couldn't begin to understand.

Focus, Ellie. I told myself. *Just focus.*

I dragged my backpack to the hole dug into the rocks.

From inside the backpack, I withdrew a silk pillowcase, the end knotted tight. The skull and bones were inside. Allison had donated the pillowcase as a way of showing respect for the remains. Best we could do in a pinch.

The shadows drew close around me, vague figures in the fog ringing me like hunters surrounding their prey.

The Trailwalker's bones clicked inside the silk pillowcase as I gently placed it inside the pit.

The figures continued to close in.

I upended my backpack, and out spilled all the little quartzite stones that had been used to make the mini-owl in the museum display. They scattered over the burlap-wrapped artifacts and silk-wrapped bones.

Then I tossed my backpack aside and eased back from the pit. My hand went automatically to my flashlight holster, but I'd lost the flashlight while crawling across the slipping, sliding rocks.

So I stayed there, on my hands and knees, watching.

The Trailwalker had shifted back to the tall, fierce-looking woman I'd seen by the lake, only in greater detail than before, the apparition sharper. I could see a plate of copper shielding her chest, an obsidian knife sheathed in leather at her hip, spiraling beadwork on her high deerskin boots.

She wore gemstone rings and seashell bangles and

woven necklaces, her clothing intricately beaded but loose and light, ideal for running the trails of Georgia's mountains.

She stared down at me, her eyes large and dark and coldly beautiful.

The ax in her hands was perfectly positioned to swing across the small pit between us, to cave in my ribs or sweep through my neck. I was at her mercy.

The shadows in the fog were clearer than ever—still featureless shades, really, but now in the shape of men and women, a group of them crowding in as if to watch my execution.

I looked up at her again.

Then I closed my eyes, whispering.

Begging for my life.

The owls, tribunes and escorts of the dead, fell silent.

After a few seconds of silence, I opened my eyes, thinking everything was fine.

Shadows charged at me from the fog.

I gasped and tried to push myself to my feet before they arrived, but there was no time.

The first shadow grabbed me.

"Ellie? Are you hurt?" It was Stacey, putting her arms around me.

Ephraim and Nathan emerged from the fog next. Their mother was yelling after them to come back, but apparently they'd been curious enough to follow Stacey. Josh appeared soon after, also yelling at the boys, carrying Shiloh in his arms.

I shivered, trying to catch my breath, too frightened to speak.

The Trailwalker was gone, though, along with the

others who'd accompanied her.

"Bury it," I said, gesturing toward the pit. "Bury it deep. And never dig it back up."

Stacey helped me to my feet and led me off the owl, as the guys began shoveling the rocks back into place, burying the Trailwalker for good.

Chapter Twenty-Eight

The rest of the day went a bit easier.

Stacey and I stopped by the dining hall and fortified ourselves with cold cereal and bottles of orange juice. We sat surrounded by rows of long, empty tables.

"Is it just me, or does the place feel different now?" Stacey asked. "The walk back wasn't the same as the walk up. And not just because of the fog lifting."

"I wish the fog would lift from my brain." I yawned, trying to crack a particularly stubborn frosted mini-wheat with the edge of my spoon. "It's been a long day and it's not even noon."

"Do you really think we settled all the hauntings by pacifying the Trailwalker?" Stacey asked. "And do you think I can find boots like hers somewhere?"

"Doubtful on the second question. And I don't know about the first. We'll keep monitoring for activity for the next couple of nights, have Jacob check the place over if he comes up this weekend. In the meantime, we'll keep looking through our data and see if we missed anything."

"And what will we do with Reverend Carmody's ghost?" Stacey asked. "Bury him?"

"Maybe." I yawned. "I definitely want to get back to the cabin soon. Let's make sure we're all set up for tonight."

We had some stops to make before we rested, like the lodge attic to make sure our gear was ready to catch any return of the boys, or of Reverend Carmody. We believed Carmody's ghost to be in our trap, but perhaps we were wrong. Other entities had been active up there.

At Bobcat Cabin, we boosted the amount of recording gear; if the boys and Gwendolyn emerged again, we certainly wanted evidence of it.

Maybe it was my imagination, but the campground did have a different feeling. Less dark and heavy, more sunny and open. It felt like we'd made real progress.

Exhausted, we treated ourselves to a trip to the bathhouse—well, I'm not sure that a brick-walled shower with a concrete drainhole floor could ever be considered a real treat, but it was getting familiar, and sort of weirdly pleasant despite the rustic conditions.

"Maybe we should try the girls' bathhouse next time," Stacey suggested as we showered. I agreed.

We slept in the afternoon.

By evening, rain pattered on the roof, waking me gently. I took a deep breath, lying comfortable in my bunk in my frayed checkerboard-pattern cotton pajamas.

Feeling unhurried, I stood and stretched. The world outside the window was purple with twilight, the trees looking lush and bright in the rainfall. Water coursed off the other cabins and in little streams throughout the campground, as though baptizing the whole place, clearing out the spiritual debris. Or maybe I was reading too much into all that.

I turned to Stacey in her bunk, thinking of waking her, but didn't. She was resting peacefully, her long blonde bangs curled across her face, making her look almost childlike and innocent, at least at this particular moment, though she was only four years younger than me.

Then she sucked some of her hair up her nostril and began coughing and hacking like a heavy smoker with lungworms, ruining that momentarily cute image.

She turned over and went back to sleep. I couldn't help feeling some warmth as I looked at her. I'd initially resisted when my boss Calvin hired her, but he'd wanted to move on, to retire, and he didn't want me hunting ghosts alone.

I was glad to have Stacey in my life. I didn't have a lot of friends, but she had definitely turned into one.

In the other bedroom, I looked at the multiple feeds from Bobcat Cabin. Despite our increased monitoring, we were getting nothing at the moment. No signs of activity yet, but the night was young.

Eventually, I grew restless and pulled up the previous night's recording from the lodge attic. A cold spot had approached the trap, vanishing when the trap snapped closed. It looked like we had snagged the preacher's ghost, but I still wasn't eager to go check in person, considering how my last encounter in the attic had gone.

The rain poured down heavier and thicker, falling in sheets and curtains outside the cabin. I resolved to stay in rather than go back up to the lodge and check those recordings like I'd planned. Not until the weather calmed down. Probably not until morning. There was no rush.

"Hey, did I miss anything?" Stacey wandered drowsily into the room, her hair in blonde clumps. At least it was out of her nose.

"Not at all," I said. "I watched a whole lot of nothing happen on the live feed. I think we really altered the situation here."

"Oh, good." She stretched and yawned. "So is it leaning toward case closed?"

"Too early to tell, but it's possible. I hope so. I'm ready to get back to my apartment, in my own bed with my own cat. Every day I'm gone is a bigger cat-sitting bill."

"Yeah, when I get home, I'm picking up an iced latte from Sentient Bean and hanging out at the park. Soaking up the everyday sights of being home. These out-of-town jobs really take it out of you—"

A shriek pierced the air, crackling over a speaker.

"What was that?" Stacey looked at the monitors with me, peering into the different rooms of Bobcat Cabin.

The signal rippled and crackled on every monitor. More shrieks sounded from the speakers; not voices, but electrical interference.

One by one, the monitors went dark, and the speakers went silent.

"Stacey?"

"I can't fix this!" She tapped at her laptop in frustration. "They shut down remotely. Like something slurped the batteries dry. Again."

"This is really bad." I looked at one monitor that was still up. It showed the feed from a night vision camera that stood in the common room of our cabin, looking out through a window at Bobcat Cabin.

The front door of Bobcat Cabin swung open as though blown by a wind from inside the cabin. It commenced banging against the outside of the cabin, as it had done incessantly on previous nights.

"It's happening again, isn't it?" Stacey whispered.

"Tonight's different. No horsing around. No giggling."

I grabbed a flashlight and walked out the front door, stopping under the shallow shelter of the overhang. Rain poured in a solid waterfall off the roof, just inches from my face.

A chain of lightning added extra visibility for a moment, but even with that dash of heavenly help, there wasn't much to see but rainwater gushing from the cabins' downspouts.

"So what do we do, captain?" Stacey asked. "Sail into the storm? Hoist the cannons? Shiver the timbers? I'm running out of nautical terms, but it's wet out here, that's what I'm saying. Too bad I didn't bring a kayak, because I could just about surf that mud flow over to Bobcat Cabin —"

"Maybe we should go to the lake," I said. "Gwendolyn drowned in a storm, and so did Josh's three friends—"

Searing light filled the whole area, and I recoiled against the cabin door, thinking the lightning had come fatally close.

"I think those are headlights," Stacey said calmly, making me look bad.

"Headlights? There's no road nearby, why would there be—"

But there were indeed highlights, high beams, projected by a vehicle that had gone completely off-road, sliding through mud, nearly plowing into Falcon Cabin before swerving at the last second. There was no road in the cabin area at all, just footpaths.

Allison's SUV came sliding to a halt not far from us, spraying a great wave of mud that soaked me from head to toe.

"Allison?" I stepped forward on the cabin's little front stoop for a closer look.

More lightning popped and crackled as the driver-side window lowered. Allison drove. Nobody was in the shotgun seat. The side of the car was badly scraped, the windows cracked. Allison had driven through a few trees on her way here.

"It came back," Allison said. "It came back to our house, Ellie. And it took my child."

Chapter Twenty-Nine

We were pretty much in five-alarm mode after that.

"We have to get to the lake!" I shouted at Allison through the roaring wind and hammering rain.

"Josh and Ephraim are on their way there!" she shouted back.

I nodded. "Give us five seconds!"

"Hurry!" she shouted as Stacey and I ran back into the cabin.

There was no time to spare, so I grabbed my backpack and a couple of things, including my boots, which I did not have time to actually put on. I didn't even grab socks.

Back outside, Stacey and I climbed into the back seat of the SUV with Shiloh; either one of us running around to the front passenger door would have wasted precious seconds.

Shiloh stopped crying when she saw me beside her—

probably not comforted, but maybe distracted for half a second.

"Your feet are muddy," she said.

I looked down, and indeed they were, soaking what would likely be permanent footprints into the carpet.

"Sorry," I said.

Allison punched the accelerator before Stacey could even close the door. We slalomed wildly through rain and mud, past the rest of the cabins, miraculously crashing into none of them before plunging ahead through a trail that was definitely not wide enough for the vehicle.

A low limb smashed against the passenger side of the windshield; it puckered inward, spider-webbing, and I was glad Stacey and I were in the back.

"What exactly happened at your house?" I asked Allison.

"It came in again. The tall one with the antlers. I saw it —*her*—more clearly than ever. She was in my room, staring at me. She shattered my bedroom window, that's how I woke up.

"Then she walked toward the kids' rooms. I screamed at Josh to wake up and then I went after her.

"I saw her go into Nathan's room. When I followed her in, she was gone, but Nate was gone, too. His window was open and the screen was broken off. The rain was pouring in all over the carpet."

"Maybe it was Gwendolyn's ghost," I said. "She might have come to his window."

"Like in Josh's story," Stacey said.

At Josh's name, Allison's shoulders hunched, her hands like fists on the wheel.

Branches and undergrowth scraped and scratched at

every side of the car, and Shiloh started crying again.

"It's, uh, going to be fine," I said, in a clearly unconvincing way, as tree limbs like giant claws raked the window beside the upset little girl.

The SUV slid sideways through the mud and smacked hard against a massive old beech tree. Allison pressed the accelerator, but the tires spun uselessly.

"We're stuck," I said. "We have to get out and run."

Shiloh unbuckled from her car seat and scrambled up to the front to her mother, crying. Allison held her.

The beech tree blocked the back door on Stacey's side, so I crawled over the car seat and out into the storm. Stacey was right behind me.

"I'm running ahead," I told Stacey. "You stay with Allison and Shiloh."

Stacey nodded; the buddy system was important, but not as important as protecting the clients.

I clomped through the mud, barely able to see through the downpour even with my flashlight and the lightning popping overhead, dangerously close. The storm was only growing worse.

Slipping and sliding, and falling more than once, I made my way through the little activity village, toward the boathouse and the dock.

The light inside the boathouse was on, glowing bright and yellow through the open door like a beacon in the storm.

I staggered inside, dripping mud from my soggy pajamas, their checkerboard pattern now completely brown.

Josh and Ephraim were scrambling to grab a canoe from the wall.

"I'm here," I gasped, as if they'd been waiting for me. "Have you seen Nathan?"

"He's out on the water," Josh said. His face was pale white. "Went right into the storm. Didn't even listen when I yelled at him. It was just like... before." His hands shook badly as he heaved the canoe. "I've been telling him and telling him to stay away from the lake."

"We'll come with you." I grabbed life vests and oars and followed them into the rain.

Stacey arrived with Allison, who carried Shiloh but struggled to keep her grip on the drenched, panicked girl. Allison set her down in the shelter of the boathouse doorway.

"Nate's out on the water." I gave Stacey an oar and a vest. To Allison and Shiloh, I said, "You two stay inside the boathouse. Keep every light on, inside and out."

Allison nodded. "Be careful."

Stacey and I hurried to the shore with Josh and Ephraim. Stacey was far more experienced than me with this kind of boating, but I wasn't going to send her out there into the center of the danger without me. I didn't like leaving Allison and Shiloh unprotected, though. Every option felt wrong.

Josh and Ephraim climbed into the canoe while Stacey and I strapped on our vests.

While I'd been caught out in my checkerboard pajamas after falsely expecting a quieter, cozier kind of rainy night, Stacey was more ridiculously clad in her snoring-Garfield boxer shorts and matching orange top. She was muddy from her feet to her knees; she wasn't wearing shoes, which seemed wise, so I kicked off my boots. If we ended up swimming, she was much luckier in her choice of sleepwear. My jammies would only slurp up water and drag me down.

We waded out and climbed into the canoe. Three of us started rowing right away, with practiced ease. I was the fourth. The others kept yelling instructions to correct my attempts at rowing, but it was hard to hear over the wind and thunder. At some point, it was determined that I should hold my flashlight to illuminate the way forward rather than try to help with the canoeing.

The water was choppy, with large swells that reminded me of the ocean, too large for such a small lake.

"Lake level's rising!" Josh yelled. "It hasn't been this high all year!" Behind us, the dock looked like a wooden sidewalk, the lake leaking up through the floorboards.

Lightning struck much too close, hitting a tree out along the shoreline with a sound like a cracking whip, reminding me that we were breaking all basic safety precautions and basic common sense about what to do in a thunderstorm.

In that moment, we spotted Nate near the center of the lake, unaware of us because of the noise and power of the storm, or too absorbed in his own purpose to care.

"That's the Cold Hole!" Josh said. "Faster! Nathan, come back!"

The choppy water worked against us, high swells shoving the canoe back, as if the lake had a mind of its own and wanted to stop us from catching up to Nathan.

Ahead, a second canoe appeared, chunky and wooden instead of colorful and polyethylene like Nate's and our own. A figure stood atop it, tall, her face in shadow under the brim of a campaign hat, a cocky smile on her lips, her wet, blonde hair trailing out behind her in the wind.

She wore a long skirt over bare feet, her toes gripping the upper rim of her canoe as it bobbed and rocked in the storm. Everything about her was unnaturally pale, as if lifted from a black and white movie, from the hat down to the canoe.

"Is that her?" I asked Josh.

He gaped at the figure ahead, the one now beckoning to his son.

Nathan stood up in his own canoe, as if to greet her and also show that he wasn't afraid. As if she'd been daring him to stand in his boat in the storm. He struggled to stay upright as the canoe rose and fell in storm-tossed water.

The figure's campaign hat blew off her head, revealing a pretty face. Her clothes were as Josh had described in his story, plastered against her, unbuttoned here and sagging there, a powerful lure to an impulsive boy.

Nate tried to paddle closer to her while standing and maintaining his balance in the storm.

His canoe overturned and he plunged into the lake.

The girl's canoe sank silently into the water beside him; she rode it down almost like an elevator, her eyes fixed on Nate as he spluttered in the water.

She reached out toward him.

"Leave him alone!" Josh shouted while I centered my light on the apparition. She hissed and faded, sinking chin-deep into the water, but unfortunately did not go away.

"Gwendolyn Malloy, get away from him!" I snapped. My use of her name drew her attention for a moment, but she wasn't taking any orders from me.

Nathan struggled and went under. He burst out, gasping for air for a second, then got pulled under again.

Gwen's face remained out of the water, her blonde hair

floating around her in pale streams. Her eyes glared at us.

"Let him go!" Josh shouted. "Take me if you have to take someone."

"You?" Gwen giggled, the sound of the invisible giggler I'd been hearing all along. "But you're too old, Joshy-Josh. This one here is just right. He'll fit in with the other boys. Maybe he'll even be my favorite, for a while."

Nathan surfaced, gasping again. She clapped a pale hand over his face and shoved him back down underwater.

"Stop!" Josh paddled harder, giving our canoe an extra burst of speed.

"Are you jealous, Joshy?" Gwen said. "Do you miss your friends? They don't miss you. You left them here. You let them die out here."

Three pairs of pale, bloated, waterlogged hands reached over the edge of the canoe.

"What is that?" Ephraim smacked his oar at one bloated hand. The hand ruptured and leaked dark lake water into our boat, but it didn't let go.

The six pale hands pulled the side of the canoe down, overturning us and dropping us into the lake, the living joining the dead in the water as rain poured down and lightning cracked across the sky.

Chapter Thirty

I bobbed and flailed, my thick jammies weighing me down, though at least I was trading campground mud for lake water.

I'm a good swimmer, but the life jacket was an unfamiliar distraction. I struggled to hold onto my backpack. My flashlight was a lost cause, already a distant glimmer far below the surface.

"Paul?" Josh gasped.

A boy was climbing on Josh, one of the boys who'd tipped our canoe. He was bloated, misshapen, like a pale leech attached to Josh's back.

"You're a coward, Josh," the dead boy said. The loose teeth in his rotten gums clicked and clacked when he talked. "You sat and watched. Stupid, crying coward."

"Get off me!" Stacey struggled with a bloated dead boy of her own, trying to drag her underwater.

Ephraim grappled with a third dead boy. All the Bobcat boys were here, in something of a dead camper zombie apocalypse.

Stacey, Ephraim, and Josh each had life preservers keeping them up, while Nathan was trapped underwater without one. I had to help Nathan first.

"I brought you something, Gwen," I said, swimming toward her. I had a gambit to try here, but no idea if it would work or not. Gwen's face was half-submerged in the water, her wide-brimmed hat restored to her head and casting her eyes in shadow, but she was definitely watching me.

The water beside her burbled and frothed as Nathan struggled but failed to break through to the surface.

I drew the ghost trap out of my backpack and opened it.

Then I hurled all of Carmody's grave dirt at Gwendolyn, pelting her with a hundred little bits of earth and dried plant, not that any of it really touched her. It sprinkled the water all around her.

Gwen's face rose all the way from the water and she snarled. "You!"

Nathan burst through the lake's surface and took a deep breath. I'd distracted Gwen's ghost for a moment, getting Nathan a reprieve for air, but it might not last.

The preacher, Reverend Roger Carmody, barely had time to form the thinnest, waxiest of apparitions before Gwen leaped on him and shoved him under the water. I could see his ghostly face through the surface, eyes wide as she drowned him.

Again.

"You were the one who attacked me in the bath,

Gwendolyn," I said, as though it had been a certainty on my part all along, when it had been more of a suspicion. I'd made preparations based on it, though. "I thought it was the preacher at first, but it was you. Your fingers didn't feel like they belonged to a burly ex-soldier like Carmody when you were holding me underwater. I've had time to think about that.

"You drowned the preacher, didn't you, Gwendolyn? *After* you died. He was your first kill as a ghost. You couldn't get to Terrance or Laurie Ann, the people who truly betrayed you, because they'd fled the camp. Once you realized what you could do, what you had the power to do in your new life as an evil spirit, it was too late. The victims you wanted were gone. The preacher was the next best thing, the only available target tied to Laurie Ann. Maybe killing him would hurt her somehow. Or maybe you just like killing. Some do, once they get a taste for it."

Gwen stared at me. Behind her, Nathan treaded water, taking deep gasps of air.

Stacey, Josh, and Ephraim were still struggling with the trio of dead boys. I needed to move fast.

"The broken oar," I said, "and the scar on Terrance's chin. Those made me think. I began to think, maybe you didn't kill yourself, and you weren't murdered, either. Maybe you tried to murder Terrance. You were going to knock him out with the oar, then fill his pockets with rocks so he'd sink in the lake. That way you didn't have to face the humiliation of breaking off the engagement you'd been so pleased about. Or the other humiliation of marrying a man you knew was unfaithful."

"Terrance... total snake," Stacey managed to gasp, from where she struggled with a badly decayed dead boy trying to drag her below.

"But it went wrong," I continued. "Maybe you didn't knock him out. Maybe you fell out of the canoe in the storm. Or maybe there was a struggle, and he pushed you.

"However it went, *you* ended up at the bottom of the lake by accident, didn't you, Gwen? Your murder plot backfired and you died instead. The rocks you were going to sink him with ended up sinking you instead.

"Then later, as the ghost you are now, you killed the preacher in his bath."

Gwendolyn glared.

"You never got what you wanted, revenge on Terrance and Laurie Ann," I said. "But there's no reason to take it out on innocent boys."

"They're not innocent," Gwendolyn said, her voice like glass and ice, as harsh as her shrieking laugh. "None of them. But they *are* mine. I can have any boy I want. Like this one."

She seized Nate's face again and shoved him back under water.

Smiling at me, she sank away after him.

There was no sign of the preacher; maybe the repeat of his death had sent him packing for now. I hadn't expected much out of him, but I'd hoped for more of a delay and distraction than he'd actually provided.

I swam to where Gwen and Nathan had gone under, but I couldn't see them from the surface. Reaching underwater, I felt nothing.

They were heading down deep.

I didn't have any choice but to unfasten my life jacket and slide out of it so I could swim down after them. So I did that, still wishing I'd slept in lighter clothes like Stacey, because these pajamas were a serious drag on my movements.

I went down and down, into water so cold I thought I might die of hypothermia, if I didn't drown or get struck by lightning. We'd found the deep part of the lake, the Cold Hole.

Lightning briefly illuminated this cold underwater realm, and I saw Nathan below me, still sliding away deeper as if tied to an anchor.

I grabbed him by the shoulder, and his hand grabbed my arm.

I couldn't pull him up; instead, he dragged me down with him.

Kicking and fighting, I discovered there wasn't much I could do to reverse course. I held on tight, hoping my presence was at least slowing him down, but I was otherwise useless.

A cold hand closed around my other arm.

Gwendolyn, her face swollen, bruise-colored, rotten, waterlogged, her smile wide. She was glad to have both of us, I supposed, two new souls for her collection, making her a stronger entity than ever. Her blonde hair and her khaki skirt swirled around her in the depths of the lake.

My lungs burned. My head felt like it was being crushed. The world was going dark. I refused to let go of Nate, though. I would try to save the poor guy with the last of my air, the last of my strength.

The water was freezing cold, and my movements became languid, weak, useless.

I was going to die trying to haul this kid up.

Gwendolyn's ghost pulled Nathan and me down into the cold slush of the lake's muddy bottom. We were far below the surface, and I didn't see any way out.

It wasn't completely dark down here, though. My flashlight, my trusty sidearm, had preceded us and was still glowing underwater. It only created a small spotlight in the gloom, but I was glad to find it.

I released Nathan, since my grip on him was plainly not doing him much good, and grabbed up the flashlight. Between my waterlogged pajamas and the pressure of all the cold water on top of us, I felt like I was moving in painfully slow motion.

My plan was to jab the intense full-spectrum white light into Gwen's face, because ghosts typically hate that, but then something glinted in my flashlight beam, drifted around in the mud our arrival had churned up here on the lake bottom.

I stared. It wasn't possible.

It was small. Metal.

A golden ring, inset with an impressively large diamond.

I closed my hand around it and gripped it tight.

Gwen's gaze instantly locked onto my closed fist, her eyes bulging and mouth open. She released her grip on Nathan and charged toward me.

Nathan could have, and should have, kicked free and swam up, using whatever reserves he had left to try and reach the surface.

Instead, the Boy Scout wrapped his arms around me, trying to take me with him. I wanted him to leave, to save himself, but we couldn't exactly speak. My chest was wracked with pain from the lack of air, and my brain was going sluggish and dark; he couldn't have had more air than me, probably less since he'd been dragged under while I'd at least taken a deep breath first. Maybe he'd had a chance to do that.

While Nate tried to pull me up, Gwen's grip tightened on my bicep, her slender, sharp fingers biting into my arm. She was determined to claim at least one victim tonight. She held me down, resisting Nate's futile attempts to save me.

Desperate, I simply punched Gwen's ghost in the face, my fist closed around the long-lost ring.

She went formless, turning into a pale underwater glow, and Nathan and I were free.

We kicked off and swam toward the surface, using air and strength we didn't really have, tapping into our bodies' last resources in a desperate struggle to survive.

Something grabbed my ankle. Gwen—I recognized the grip of her slender, sharp, cold fingers by now.

Nathan continued upward. I hoped he would remain unaware of my predicament and save himself. I'd only dived down here in the first place to try to save him; if we both ended up dead, I would be seriously annoyed about it.

Gwen glared up at me, her face glowing soft and blue under the water, her teeth bared. She was beautiful, demonically so, alluring as a fallen angel.

She probably wanted the ring in my hand, but if I reached the surface with the ring in my possession, I could use it to lure her into a ghost trap. That was my new plan: step one, don't drown; step two, bait a trap for Gwen, at some point after succeeding at step one, which was definitely top priority.

Maybe she would have let me go if I'd released the ring, but I knew if I dropped it, there was little chance of anyone ever finding it again. For the sake of my clients, I needed to remove the ring from the lake, not return it into the lake's depths.

I struck at her face again; the ring in my fist seemed to give me some real power over her. My knuckles smashed into slimy, deathly cold skin and a sharp, high cheekbone.

She released me, but only to surge up alongside me, giving me a hateful smile as I tried to resume my struggle to the surface.

Her fingers closed around my mouth and nose, gripping my face.

I punched her again, but it was feeble. I had no more oxygen, no more power to put into it.

She knew it, too. I could tell by the way she smiled, her face close to mine, her dead blue eyes watching me die.

Then those triumphant eyes of hers went wide with distress.

Her chest thrust forward and ruptured, the sharp edge of an ax blade jutting out. Inky black blood crawled out like a mass of worms in the water around her, as if her stricken heart had released its inner darkness.

Gwen was dragged up toward the surface like a fish on the end of a spear.

I was limp. No air left, no strength, floating in the dark depths like a spirit between worlds, not sure whether I would sink or rise, but powerless to affect my fate. Whatever strength I'd had, I'd spent it all fighting Gwen.

Nathan had made it up, though. I had not failed in my job. I could cross to the next world secure in that knowledge.

Arms embraced me. Hands gripped me, strong and sure.

I rose rapidly through the water, hauled up by an

unseen benefactor. She was female, I could tell from her touch. Her long, decorated braids of hair floated around my face, brushing me with glittering gemstones, pointy seashells, and bits of metal.

As we approached the surface, another shape swam down from above and seized me. This one was much more solid, definitely male and among the living, and he hauled me the rest of the way up into the glorious, life-giving world of air above.

I burst out above the water and sucked in a long, deep desperate pull of air, telling myself I would never again take air for granted or fail to appreciate the wonder and glory of readily available air.

Nathan, who'd dived back down and dragged me up that last leg of my journey, held me as I coughed up cold, thick water from the lake's bottom.

I looked around to see the other person, the one who'd brought me all the way up from the depths, but there was no one I could see. I'd had a feeling there wouldn't be.

Nathan took in a sharp breath. He stared, aghast, at something above us.

Gwen's apparition hung like a limp corpse, her torso impaled on the business end of an ax with a handle as long as a canoe oar.

The Trailwalker held the long ax. She stood in a canoe built from what had once been an immense tree trunk, adorned with spirals and fish shapes, a royal boat, definitely the largest craft on the lake that night. A copper breastplate gleamed on the Trailwalker's chest, etched with a horned owl emblem, its wings outstretched in flight. She looked more human than ever, though clearly still not of this world, not for a long time.

She'd caught Gwen and hauled her out of the water, and now inspected her like a speared fish bleeding its life back into the water.

"No," Gwen gasped, twitching, looking in horror at the ancient ax head protruding from her chest, suspending her above the lake.

The scene terrified me. My fist tightened around the ring I clutched; the diamond bit into the soft flesh of my palm.

Shadows moved on either side of the Trailwalker, the dead queen's entourage standing in the ancient boat with her. They threw out dark lines of braided rope that coiled around Gwen, binding her, making her their prisoner.

"No!" screamed the ghost of Gwen, the young murderess struggling to be free. She screamed again until one of the vine ropes snapped across her mouth, silencing her.

The queen's shadowy hunters pulled Gwen into their boat and bound her tight, like a prey animal they'd caught, and would perhaps be gutting and devouring later.

Another shadowy figure rose from below the water to join the crew. I couldn't see this apparition well, but her long, heavily decorated braids told me this was my unseen benefactor who'd rescued me up from below. One of the dead queen's ghostly entourage, perhaps a soldier, certainly a great swimmer. The Trailwalker had sent her to help me. Good thing we'd restored the Trailwalker's remains to her burial site.

"Thank you," I said to my faceless benefactor, who was so thin and shadowy I could barely see her. If she responded to my gratitude, I couldn't tell. I also thanked the Trailwalker. She looked down at me impassively.

Regally.

The dead queen turned her gaze away, and her shadowy crew of ghosts dropped their oars to the water. They advanced toward Stony Owl Hill in the distance.

In another flash of lightning, they were gone.

As the lightning faded, deafening thunder echoed back and forth across the sky, like a bellowing shout ricocheting down a vast canyon.

"Are you okay?" I asked Nathan, whose arm was still supporting me.

"Not really," he gasped. "Alive, though. My dad was...right. I should have stayed away from the lake."

"Thanks for coming back for me," I told him.

"Hey, you did it for me. Just so you know, I was ready to give you mouth to mouth, too, if you needed it. I've got the lifesaving merit badge."

"I bet." I pulled away from him, treading water on my own now.

I'd last seen Stacey, Josh, and Ephraim struggling against three dead boys. Those dead boys were still in the water, but had moved away from the living people they'd been attacking. They huddled together, shivering, no longer looking monstrous. Looking like boys who'd gone out for a night of fun and seen it turn into a spectacle of horror.

"I'm sorry," Josh said. "Thomas. Paul. Kyle. I should have gone with you."

"You were always with us," one of them said.

"You still are," said another.

A fourth boy appeared among the others, paler and blurrier than the others, like a nearly forgotten memory.

"That's... me," Josh said, as the boy figure swam closer to him. "That's what I left behind here. What I've been missing."

The fourth ghost boy vanished as it reached Josh.

Josh took a deep breath and straightened up, as if rejuvenated, a long-lost piece of himself returned.

"What now?" Josh asked his deceased friends. "What should I do? Paul? You always had the ideas. Not always the safest ones, obviously—"

"Boys!" A stern voice called from the shore. Reverend Carmody stood there in his campaign hat and khaki camp uniform. He didn't look recently drowned, or even wet. He looked as if he, too, had been restored somehow. "Boys, we're late! Let's hit the trail!"

The three boys looked at him. They shared a little smile among themselves, then swam toward the shore, racing each other to where the original owner and director of the camp waited to guide them to their next activity, whatever that might have been.

Then they were all gone, every single ghost, leaving us five living people treading water among overturned canoes and waterlogged pajamas.

I opened my hand. The moonlight reflected off the sizable diamond on Gwendolyn Malloy's engagement ring. It must have slipped off the night she'd drowned—or perhaps she'd removed it and dramatically flung it away into the water when she'd confronted Terrance about his cheating ways with the preacher's wife.

Regardless, it had lain at the bottom of the lake all these years, an emotionally charged artifact of Terrance's betrayal, of Gwen's initial hopeful happiness at being engaged to him, followed by her humiliation at her fiance's hands, then her subsequent murderous fury. The ring might have helped anchor her ghost to the campground as she stalked its trails, restless and malevolent.

I'd been lucky to find it down at the lake bottom after so many years.

Or maybe, like my last-minute lift to the surface, it had been more than luck. Maybe the ancient local spirits had made sure I found the ring for a reason: because they wanted the cursed diamond ring gone, its dark magic removed from their sacred land forever.

Chapter Thirty-One

I sealed Gwendolyn's engagement ring in a ghost trap. The plan was to swing by Valdosta on our way home—not that it was really on the way home, but it "kinda-sorta" was, as Stacey put it. We'd discreetly bury the ring in the soil at her grave; hopefully no groundskeepers would catch us in the act.

Before any of that, Stacey and I stayed on at the campground an extra couple of days to make sure we'd truly cleared out the haunting. All seemed calm, but we'd been wrong before.

We helped with a pleasant daytime project that originated with an idea from Shiloh, who'd said "the people in the woods" might be happiest if we planted some of their favorite plants around Stony Owl.

The family tilled the soil along the inside of the chain-link fence surrounding the ancient effigy. Guided by

archaeological research, we set out sunflowers, a major local
food source in ancient times, as well as mulberry trees,
grapevines, a trellis with strawberries and blackberries, a
few hazelnut and chinquapin shrubs for nuts, and more.
There would be fruits and flowers aplenty to feed the local
birds and wildlife... and the owls who preyed upon them.

By late afternoon, everyone was dirty, sweaty, and worn
out. The place was looking great, though, a garden oasis.
The weeds around the owl had been mowed nice and short,
too.

"Not a bad start," Josh said, wiping his dirty face on his
sleeve. "Now we can go up in the tower for a real bird's eye
view, huh?"

His sons groaned and shook their heads at the idea of
hiking up the winding tower stairs.

Allison cut him a burning look. She was still
understandably angry at him for holding back so much of
the past from her. That was going to take a while to heal.
Fortunately, I didn't have to stick around for that drama.
Just take your check and leave town, that's how private
investigators get to play it.

"The people in the woods are quiet now," Shiloh said,
looking out the open fence. "They like the plants. They'll
keep us safe from the bad things, as long as we're good.
We're good, right, Mommy?"

Allison nodded. "I think so. We're not so bad, at least."
She looked at me and Stacey. "Thanks for all your help."

"No problem," I said, still trying to calculate their final
bill. "We should be able to wrap up over the weekend."

"So what's the fate of Camp Stony Owl?" Stacey asked.
"Do y'all think it's safe to open this summer?"

"We'll get it inspected if we do. Multiple times." Allison

glanced at Josh, who nodded, abashed.

"I think we should," Ephraim said. "We got rid of the bad ghosts, right? And we put all this work into it."

"Hey, I nearly died here," Nate said. "But it was kind of cool. I mean, the good ghosts saved me, and that evil ghost girl was also totally hot and really into me. Obviously she was never going to go for Effie—"

"Don't," Ephraim said.

"Probably that other ghost chick with the antlers was into me, too," Nathan said. "That's why she saved us. Good thing it wasn't Effie, because she probably wouldn't have bothered—"

"Shut up!"

"Next time, wear a life vest," Stacey said. "And use the buddy system. And don't go out on the water in a storm. I cannot emphasize this stuff enough."

Nate nodded. So did Josh, or at least he gave the ghost of a nod.

We started down the hill together, and the woods were serene.

Chapter Thirty-Two

"This place is positively haunted," Jacob said as we approached the chain-link gate to the owl effigy.

"Really?" Stacey groaned. "After all that work we did?"

"Ghosts?" Michael said, pretending to be scared. "Nobody said anything about ghosts!"

"I'll protect you." I took his hand with my non-flashlight one.

Michael had surprised me by riding up with Jacob from Savannah. As far as we could tell, the case was closed, but a sign-off from a reliable psychic was needed here. That was Jacob.

Stacey had secretly arranged for Michael to come with him; the idea was we could all enjoy a weekend at the camp together, which is a thing many people apparently do for recreation, so I went along with it. Just a couple of ghost trappers and their boyfriends.

It was around midnight on Friday, and the guys had arrived in time for a moonlit walk where Jacob could put out his psychic feelers all over the campground. The moonlight was so strong we barely needed flashlights.

Now we stood at the gate to the effigy mound, and Jacob had made a most unfortunate pronouncement.

"I mean, they're a positive presence," he said. "It's gentle. Like the background noise of the owls up there. There was something here long ago..." He shook his head.

"Will this help?" I unlocked the gate with my borrowed key and opened it wide.

Jacob took a deep breath and nodded as he looked at the effigy. He made no move to go inside the fence, despite the open gate.

A long minute passed. Maybe two or three, I didn't track it. I looked up at Michael; I was still a little flushed with excitement from his surprise appearance. Maybe another night at the campground wouldn't be so bad. We could pick any cabin we wanted.

"It's fine," Jacob finally said. "They're content as long as they're treated with respect. Leave the gate closed except for gardening. These aren't spirits your clients need to worry about. They could actually help against more negative influences. But this area here..." He gestured at the Stony Owl effigy. "Needs to be respected. Otherwise things could go wrong."

"No kidding," Stacey said, drawing a questioning look from Jacob, but she didn't elaborate.

"This area has a strong, strange energy. The old spirits left a little of themselves here as permanent guardians of it."

"We need to know how they feel about living people

coming here," I said. "Do they want this whole area left vacant? Or is it okay if Josh and Allison revive the campground?"

Jacob looked into the fence, then shrugged. "Just stay out of here." He stepped forward and began to close the gate. "They have a positive outlook on the camp, because the camp is mostly children, mostly innocents."

"Good enough for me." I locked the gate.

"There's a lot of thin trace apparitions here," Jacob said as we all started down the hill together. "Not surprising, I guess, if people have lived here so long. What's weird is the sort of basic, calm happiness of it. All the little ghosts of the past, all the little parts of themselves that people left here—pieces of their childhood, you know—those are still here. And they're a little extra charged up, because this was a sacred place. It was long ago, and still is."

I felt relieved as we walked down the hill. This had been a strange case, certainly. There was magic in these hills, as so many former campers recalled fondly, even in the darkest times.

We passed the lake. Jacob glimpsed a few boys and girls out there, seen only to him, but they vanished as quickly as he described them. "They seem happy enough, too."

"Did someone order a bonfire?" Michael asked as we started up toward the trail toward our now-familiar cabin area. Glowing red light flickered ahead.

I put on speed, worried that our cabin might have somehow caught fire. Perhaps a final attack from a vengeful spirit.

We emerged into the cluster of boys' cabins to see a large fire raging. It was in the fire ring where it belonged, though, where Ephraim and Nathan now stood and called to us.

"Isn't it a little late to start a fire?" I asked, slowing to a normal walk.

"It's only one in the morning," Stacey replied. "Given our usual hours, it's almost too early."

"Hey, who wants marshmallows?" Nathan held up a bag as the four of us arrived. "Anyone? Stacey? Anyone?"

"How was the walk?" Ephraim looked at us carefully.

"Things seem fine," I replied, taking a seat on a log and accepting a marshmallow from Nathan, after he'd pressed a couple into Stacey's hands. "The local spirits are okay with the campground being revived, as long as everyone respects their area."

"That's basically what Shiloh says," Ephraim told me.

"But she's always making stuff up." Nathan looked at Jacob as if sizing him up. "So you're really Stacey's boyfriend?"

"Yep." Jacob gave him a dubious look, adjusting his thick glasses, and took one of the marshmallows.

"You must have mad game," Nathan said.

"Don't say stupid things, Nathan," Ephraim said. "Let's tell them the new story."

"What new story?" I asked, watching the marshmallow on my stick blacken beautifully.

"For when the camp opens," Ephraim said. "We figured we need a new—"

"—totally new version of the Trailwalker legend," Nate said.

"Now that we know more about her," Ephraim added.

"Oh, I definitely want to hear this." Stacey leaned against Jacob while she started to toast a marshmallow.

"Yeah, so it starts like..." Nate frowned. "You start it,

Effy."

"Don't call me that. So anyway...thousands of years ago, a powerful queen lived here, at the top of Stony Owl Hill. She ruled over all the tribes in these mountains, and she wore a crown of deer antlers. She was buried under Stony Owl, along with her favorite weapons, her obsidian knife and her ax. And sometimes, late at night, you can see her out walking the trail with her troop of ghost warriors..."

The boys passed their updated legend back and forth, one picking up whenever the other paused too long, making up the rest of it as they went.

I sat close to Michael—his smiling face a welcoming and soothing sight—and watched the smoke and embers spiral upward and vanish into the starlit sky above.

THE END

FROM THE AUTHOR

I hope you enjoyed this latest ghostly adventure with Ellie and Stacey. A few historical sites in Georgia inspired this tale, most notably Rock Eagle, located in the Chattahoochee National Forest. A large 4H campground is adjacent to the site, and like many elementary-age Georgians I spent a few nights in a cabin there as part of a school field trip. The sister site, Rock Hawk, is much less known, and I'd never heard of it before researching for this book. Another inspiration was the Etowah mounds, also in north Georgia, once home to a sizable town of hilltop buildings. The Woodland period remains a fascinating and mysterious era of ancient American history, one that left us fascinating artifacts indicating continent-wide trading networks.

Next up, Ellie and Stacey land a case back home. A quirky young family has a vision to restore a old drive-in theater that has stood abandoned for years on a highway outside Savannah, a symbol of a lost era and a forgotten time, but something evil waits in the darkness when the lights go down and the illusions light up the screen.

Come along with Ellie and Stacey as they investigate a menacing and murderous presence in the next book, *Midnight Movie*. It should be quite a show!

Printed in Great Britain
by Amazon